MW00616789

BE MY VALENTINE

A Valentine's Novella Two

Hold On To Me Series

Blue Saffire

Perceptive Illusions Publishing, Inc.

Bay Shore, New York

Blue Saffire/Perceptive Illusions Publishing, Inc.
PO BOX 5253
Bay Shore, NY 11706
www.BlueSaffire.com

Publisher's Note: This is a work of fiction. Names, characters, places, and incidents are a product of the author's imagination. Locales and public names are sometimes used for atmospheric purposes. Any resemblance to actual people, living or dead, or to businesses, companies, events, institutions, or locales is completely coincidental.

Ordering Information:
Quantity sales. Special discounts are available on quantity purchases by corporations, associations, and others. For details, contact the "Special Sales Department" at the address above.

Be My Valentine: A Valentine's Novella Book 2/ Blue Saffire. -- 1st ed.
ISBN 978-1-941924-53-2

Things change all of the time. Breathe and move through it!

—Blue Saffire

Missed Call

Cristóbal

This is my third call today and she hasn't answered a single one. My patience grows thin with this dance we're doing. This woman is playing a foolish game with me.

I growl at the sound of her voice telling me to leave a message. *Me.* I should never have to hear that message. My calls should never go unanswered.

This is my fault, I've been too lenient. Years of free reign has led to this disrespect. I tighten my fist around my phone.

Pulling the device from my ear, I dial a different number. I know I will get an answer from this line. My brother wouldn't dare ignore my calls.

"This must be my unlucky day. First, your wife, now you," he groans in greeting.

"You spoke to my wife?" I seethe.

"Just hung up with her. She needs a favor."

"Why does my wife think it's okay to ignore my calls. Yet, you have spoken to her?"

"*Hermano*, I don't get in the middle of you and your wife. I told you I didn't think it was a good idea from the beginning—"

"I'm not asking you for advice, Manny," I say cutting him off. "You can let my wife know that if I don't hear from her before the New Year she is cut off."

"Cristó, isn't that a bit harsh," he says.

"She knows the deal. She wants to play these games. I will play. Make sure she gets my message."

I hang up, tossing my phone on my desk and rising from my seat. I glare at my assistant, failing to reel in my temper. I've had enough.

"If she is not here by the holidays prepare for me to go to the States," I demand.

"You would run after her?" Alonso says with a hint of disapproval.

"Who the fuck are you questioning? Have I sold my *huevos* and sent out an invitation for you all to fuck me?"

"I just—"

"You will just do what I say. Christmas. I head for the States if she's not here by Christmas," I bark. I straighten my suit jacket and start out of my office. I'm still muttering to myself as I walk out of the door. "Who the fuck do they all think they're playing with."

CHAPTER ONE

Wife's Return

Cristóbal

My jaw ticks and I flex my fingers. I stare out of my office window that reveals a beautiful ocean view. It usually serves to calm me.

At the moment, it's only serving to piss me off more as memories of the last time I saw my wife come to mind. Our marriage used to be in name only. I spent eighteen years of my life married to a woman I've never touched.

When the young brown faced, pretty-eyed girl came to me at seventeen, I was intrigued. She was smart, savvy, and had the guts to come to me and demand I help her. Even if she weren't a friend of my little brother, I would have heard her out just from watching her carry herself.

"You will help," she demanded with her Jersey accent.

This tiny little girl was demanding things from me. I liked her right away. Yes, she was gorgeous even then, but I had no intention of placing a finger on her.

"And why is it you think I will help you?" I asked as I grinned at the young girl.

"Because you are my new family. I take care of my family. I make my family wealthy. You are rich and you have connections, but I will make you wealthy," she said with such confidence.

"How old are you, little girl?"

"Seventeen going on eighteen," she replied, lifting her chin. "But that doesn't matter. Give me time to show you. I'm what you need around here. I can take your operation in the States to new levels."

I gave her a full belly laugh, but I also give her a year to prove herself. That little brown girl proved herself all right. Within two months, she improved her broken American Spanish and became fluent in the dialect of my family here in Puerto Rico.

She ran my men as if they were her own. Before I knew it she had become Manny's right hand. I never had a second thought of taking her under my wing. I taught her and she taught me. She earned my respect.

"They don't respect me." She stormed into my office with her fist clenched. "You asked me to do a job and I have done it, but not without disrespect I don't deserve."

I looked up from the reports on my desk. My fortune had tripled within the year she spent with me. I had just been thinking of her reward.

"Why do you think this is?" I asked.

"Because I'm not a Suarez," she hissed. "To them I'm the American brat. Your pet."

I stood, walking around my desk to lean against it as I folded my arms across my chest and crossed my legs at the ankles. I took in my little spitfire. She was more beautiful than when she arrived a year before with my little brother.

"So it's not because you are a woman?"

I watched her face as I asked the question. Her eyes hardened and her full lips pitched. Her small hands went to her hips.

"No," she bit out.

"And it is not because of your age?"

"Haven't I proved that my age is just a number."

"Sí, you have. How do you suggest we fix this?" I asked with a grin on my lips.

"Let me cut a few of their asses up," she said with a dark smile on her lips.

I laughed, something I didn't do with my men. Some may have thought I'd gone soft when it came to my little American. I didn't believe so. She made me sharp.

"You will keep those blades in your mouth," I say through my laughter.

"You're laughing at me. I'm serious. None of them care that I'm a woman. Well, with the expectation of when they're staring at my ass. If I were a Suarez we wouldn't be having this conservation," she said crossing her arms over her chest.

I don't know what it was about her words, but I didn't like the thought of my men looking at her ass in any way. My jaw tightened and my laughter died. A million irrational thoughts entered my head.

She was eighteen and I was thirty. She'd become a little sister, nothing more. Yet, once the idea took root I did what I'm known for. I followed my instincts.

"You and Manny will run all of this someday. You have become family. I will make sure the world respects you," I paused and narrowed my eyes. "You need to become a Suarez."

She scoffs. "And how do I do that?"

"You are here because of your father's debt back in the States," I say letting my words hang in the air. I watch as her face changes. "You thought I didn't ask questions?"

"I… I don't know what I thought," she said lifting her head higher.

"Those debts are being paid with the money you send home. I can make them go away faster," I said in offering.

There was something about her demeanor that changed at the mention of her father and his debts. I wrote it off as her being embarrassed. Maybe even scared that I wouldn't like her reasons for coming to me. Although, I hadn't seen her fear a thing since I met her.

"How?"

"You marry a Suarez, you become a Suarez. You will have the respect of a Suarez," I said, showing no emotion.

"I'm not marrying Manny," she burst into laughter.

She would think I was talking about my brother. Manny befriended this young beauty somehow while growing up with our uncle in New York. Their friendship is an unusual one.

"I never said I was speaking of Manny," I replied.

"Then who?"

"Me."

Her mouth fell open. I watched as a million thoughts ran across her face. Her tough exterior revealed a simple crack.

"You're thirty. I'm about to turn nineteen. That's just crazy."

"Don't get me wrong. You are a very attractive young woman, but this would be for business. You would be my wife in name only," I explain.

"What?"

"We will marry. You'll gain access to my money. You'll go back to the States to start this business with the friend you've told me of. You'll help Manny clean and grow my money and I will take care of all of your other problems," I said.

"You would give me money to help my family and Nelson?" Her brows knit with the words.

"Sí. What's mine will be yours. You will come to Puerto Rico twice a year. We will spend time together to talk business and make a few appearances," I said as the plan formed in my head.

"I don't get it. What do you get out of this?"

"I grow tired of the women I fuck trying to make themselves my wife. If I'm already married they will know that all they can ever have is a good time and a great fuck," I said and shrugged.

"So you would have other women?" she asked scowling at me.

"As you will be free to do as you please. My only request is that you don't embarrass me. Keep your personal life private."

"Will you do the same?"

"Your visits will be the only time I appear in public with a woman on my arm," I reassure her.

Her eyes narrowed. Meanwhile, I grew to like the idea more and more. My men would give her the respect she deserved and they wouldn't dare touch my wife.

"Is this some type of test?" she asked, that sassy New Jersey Spanglish accent coming to the surface. As usual, I got a hint of a New York flavor as well. "Why would you do this?"

"When you first arrived you told me I would help you. You were right. I'm helping you," I replied.

"Okay, I just have one request."

I still remember the grin on her face as it all sunk in. It brought me great pleasure, but not nearly as much pleasure as my last visit with my wife.

"We will need to leave in an hour, Señor Cristóbal," my assistant says pulling me from my thoughts. "Your aircraft is ready."

"I will be ready."

~B~

Detra

I fidget in my seat which is so unlike me. I've been avoiding this trip like the plague. There was a time when I had no problem returning to my husband's home for his requested two visits a year. That was before.

"Pull it together," I murmur to myself.

It's been a year since I last saw Cristóbal. A year since everything about our marriage changed. I was a fool to play with fire.

My husband may have been forty-eight, but he looked and fucked like he was in his mid-twenties. Last Christmas is one I will never forget. I wanted to show off my skills at making coquito the way my father taught me.

One thing led to another and my simple flirting turned into a fuck feast for two weeks. One morning after screaming and clawing at my husband's back all night, I woke up and I ran. Things were getting complicated.

Cristóbal has been my mentor, my friend, my family. I never meant to cross that line and take things there. For years, just his voice has had the power to make me shiver, but I chalked that up to him being one of the sexiest men I've ever met.

He could make a nun weep as she forgot her vows and threw herself at him. He has only aged like fine wine, if you can call it aging. I've slept with guys half his age and never felt the way Cristóbal made me feel.

I squeeze my thighs together just thinking about it. This is the reason I haven't returned. I've been avoiding him like the plague to keep out of his bed.

"I will take care of the bags, Señora Suarez," the driver says as he pulls to a stop.

I go to open the door to step out, but I'm frozen in place as Cristóbal storms out of the house barking orders over his shoulder. All of that power rolling off of one man should be illegal. He stops and turns to bellow something else.

I shake off my daze and step from the car. I didn't tell him that I was coming. I got his message from Manny. I knew he would send one sooner or later.

The car trunk seems to slam and ring out through the courtyard. Cristóbal spins around to find the source of the noise. His eyes lock on me and he takes my breath away. Even from this distance those hazel-blue eyes unnerve me.

It's only been a year, but his hair has more white in it overcoming the black in those thick locks. It looks stunning against his tanned skin. I was shocked last year to find he cut off all his long locks in exchange for a pompadour cut that's just as sexy on him.

He's wearing a beard that's salt and pepper in color and compliments his strong Latino features. A charcoal grey suit covers all six-two of that solid muscle and raw sex appeal.

When he lifts his hand and crooks his finger at me, my knees nearly buckle.

"Come, *Esposita*," he says in that voice that can melt the panties off of a stadium of women all at once.

I shouldn't have come. This is not going to end well. I don't know how to say no to my husband.

~B~

Cristóbal

"You haven't answered my question," I say after catching my breath.

I slap her naked ass as a smile spreads across my face. I haven't been satisfied with taking another woman to bed, I wanted my wife. One taste of Detra and I've been a starving man since she ran off a year ago.

At first, I tried to tell myself that it wasn't a big deal. She's young and we had a little fun for a few weeks. I even tried to blame my disinterest in other woman on getting old.

However, when I found myself eagerly awaiting her usual visits and she didn't show, I had to admit to myself that I only want Detra Suarez in my bed.

"How could I with your tongue down my throat?" she replies.

"I don't recall you complaining."

"Didn't say I was," she says, running her small hand over my bare chest.

"You are still avoiding my question," I say with humor.

My patience grows thin with my little wife. If I didn't crave her so much, I wouldn't have taken her to bed until I had answers. Yet, from the moment I turned to find her in my courtyard, dressed in that tight black dress and red heels, I had to have her.

She is a short but curvy woman. At least her bottom half has curves that draw the eye. Her breasts are smaller than I usually go for, but they are enough to fill my palms. That dress clung to her warm brown skin, mahogany with tones of reds and gold.

"What was the question again?" She purrs reaching to wrap my cock in her palm, stroking my semi-hard length.

I've taken her five times already and still it's not enough. When I'm with her I feel like I'm in my twenties again. I know I will take her at least twice more before I give her a break.

I reach for her hand to still it. I won't allow the distraction. I want answers.

"Why have you been avoiding my calls and why are you just returning?"

With a sigh she rolls away from me onto her back. I turn onto my side to stare down at her sexy tight body. Every inch, every ounce, and every single curve forms perfection. Her skin is so smooth, shining with our combined sweat.

"Things have been busy," she says, fidgeting under my gaze.

"You have never lied to me before. Don't start now," I retort.

"I'm not lying. Nelson and I have been working on the expansion. We needed to handle some things that came—"

"Your visits are non-negotiable. You will not miss another," I cut her off.

She frowns at me, but I'm unyielding. Placing a hand on her thick hips, I draw her closer to me. I can't keep myself from taking her full mouth.

I feel the fight leave her as I devour her lips. Twice a year will never be enough. I'm no longer content with the arrangement I made with the young and eager girl that wanted to take her rightful place in my family.

"I grow tired of this arrangement," I say against her lips.

"You want a divorce?" she asks, surprise and dare I say hurt coloring her words.

"Have I said that, *Cariño*?"

"No."

"I don't like waiting here for you to return to me when you feel like it. I want my wife with me," I say, watching her face as she takes in the words.

Her brows draw in and her brown eyes grow wide. I knew this would be her reaction. This was never supposed to happen. We were never supposed to be more than business partners.

"Cristó, are you serious? I'm not your real wife. I mean, my family has never met you. I don't do relationships," she rambles.

"You're my wife. Our marriage is very real, chica. We will bring your family here to meet me," I reply, waving off her last statement.

"Where is this coming from?"

I push a hand into the back of her hair and tug her head back. Our eyes lock and I hold her gaze. Detra is not a stupid woman. She went from being a wise young woman to a fiery and very intelligent woman that never misses a detail.

"I don't like this... this act you're playing with me. You are not a silly woman. This is why I married you and we have been friends for this long—"

"Cristó—"

"No, listen to me, *Esposita*. We have spent year after year getting to know each other. I've always looked forward to your visits. Your honesty and mind have been refreshing.

"I have valued our time as an... escape. *Sí*. That's it. *Escapar*. I have nothing but respect for you. You make me laugh and you challenge me. I don't always like this... but you would not be you if you didn't.

"I thought I would go to my grave without ever making love to my wife. That has changed. You have grown into a beautiful woman. Your body bloomed for me from the first moment I touched you. My body has craved yours since you were last in my bed." I pause to push a lock of jet black coiled hair behind her eye.

"Things have changed," I say, my eyes dropping to her lips.

"No, they haven't," she says defiantly.

The phone rings interrupting my words. I narrow my eyes at my wife as I reach for the nightstand to answer the call. This is not over by far.

"*Hola*," I grit into the phone.

"Señor, would you like me to send the dress up for Senora Suarez," Alonso says. "If you still want to attend the ball you will need to start to prepare."

"*Mierda*," I mutter. "Send it up. We will be ready."

I end the call and toss the phone down. I almost forgot that — before I carried her off to bed— I ordered my staff to get a dress for my wife to accompany me to a party this evening. Although I had planned to skip the party to head to the States, it is an event I need to show my face at.

Having Detra with me will make for a better show. Turning to her, I palm her face and take one more kiss from her seductive lips. I have to force myself not to climb over her and thrust into her tight pussy.

"This is not over, *Detrita*," I warn kissing her forehead.

CHAPTER TWO

Trophy Wife

Detra

Inside I'm a fidgeting mess, but I squish that all down for this affair. Cristóbal never shows a weakness and neither will I. I will deal with our mess when we return home.

"Ah, I have longed to see you again," a voice rings in my direction. I turn to see Jesús, one of the first men I was able to get to fall in line with my plan to expand Cristóbal's network. "You are more stunning than when I first met you."

"Jesús, you haven't aged yourself," I say as I beam at him.

"You lie, *mi amor*," he chuckles, pulling me into a hug.

He releases me and his eyes roll over my body wrapped in this tight red dress. I didn't think Cristó was going to allow me to leave in this dress from the look he gave me when I walked down the stairs to meet him.

"Do you always make it a habit to eye fuck another man's wife, *amigo*," Cristóbal says as his heat greets my back.

He hands me a glass of champagne splaying his hand over my belly once I retrieve the glass. The heat from his palm causes my belly to flip. I can't believe I still crave more of him after this morning and afternoon.

"You will have to forgive an old man, Suarez. I may have forgotten myself," Jesús says. "It was my pleasure to see you again, Detra. Enjoy the evening."

"Good to see you too, Señor Vega."

As soon as he's gone, I spin on Cristóbal. His eyes are fixed on Jesús's retreating back. I glare up at my husband.

"What was that?"

"I don't like the way he looked at you," he says and shrugs.

"Men have looked at me like that almost all of my life. You have seen this before. What's wrong with you?"

"*Sí,* they have and I never liked it. I especially don't like it now," he says tightly.

"Why is it a problem all of a sudden?"

He crowds my space, bending until he's nose to nose with me. My chest heaves with anticipation and I want to chide myself. But how can I resist those hazel-blue eyes and the smell of his cologne.

"You, *mi amor*, are playing a very dangerous game with me," he warns.

I suppress the shudder that threatens to run through me. I never thought I'd see sexy and power equate to each other in one man. Not on this level.

It isn't lost on me that he has called me his love. It's a common endearment, but not one he has ever used with me. I force myself not to follow that line of thought.

"I'm asking a legit question. Why is it a problem now?"

He cups the back of my neck, pulling me to him. The kiss he delivers is not meant for public viewing. He sucks and nips at my lips. His tongue seeking and searching in my mouth.

"Do you still have questions?" he pants.

I bite back the smart-ass reply I have on the tip of my tongue. Something in his eyes tells me this is not the time to try him. I've done enough of that tonight. Actually, for a year now.

"I don't understand why everything has to change. I like the way things were," I say instead.

He lifts my chin with his fingertips. "Are you sure? You want things to go back the way they used to be?"

I narrow my eyes at him not liking his tone one bit. I know him too well to fall for his play of words. It's one of the things that has made him an excellent businessman. He has a way of making you think everything he says is your idea.

"You want me to change everything about my life after eighteen years. I'm thirty-eight, you are forty-nine. What do we have in common that will sustain this change?

"Great sex isn't enough for me to throw my sanity away. Nor my freedom. You gave me this. Why are you trying to take it away now?" I snap.

His eyes harden and his jaw works under his beard. I can see I've pissed him off. I didn't come all this way to argue with him. I could have gone with Nelson and Talina to London if I would have known this was what I was walking into.

"So I am an old man to you that only provides you money and great sex. Staying with me is prison to you? I have seen you as more than this, *Esposita*. It is clear that I've made the mistake," he says tightly and turns to walk away.

"Cristó," I call after him.

I feel my heart sink. I didn't mean for any of that to come out the way it did. My visits have always been some of my greatest times. I looked forward to them every year. Not just because Cristóbal spoils me rotten with gifts, shopping sprees, and trips on his yacht. He has become a trusted friend. We talk about everything… well except the men I've dated and I use that term loosely.

I've had my heart broken enough to know it's not worth it. In the end, I always realize the guys were never what I thought I wanted anyway. It takes a strong man to handle me.

A man like Cristó.

I shake that thought off. I'm not looking for a relationship. Nelson wants to expand the business. Manny has asked me to come up with some new ideas for growing the family business without getting his hands any more dirty.

It's just sex.

"I have never seen the two of you so… publicly affectionate."

I turn to find Amelia. I'm pretty sure Cristó used to fuck her. I've wanted to scratch her eyes out on numerous occasions. Now, I just smile at her smugly as my eyes take in her plastic face. No wonder Cristóbal stopped seeing her.

"I'm not big on PDA," I say and shrug.

Her eyes roll over me in disdain. Like I need her damn approval. I maybe five-two and dark skinned with my Puerto Rican and Jamaican mixed heritage, but I've never let these women here make me feel less for being dark skinned.

I've heard it all. Especially after marrying Cristóbal. I got over not fitting in a long time ago. As a kid the Puerto Rican kids told me I wasn't Puerto Rican, I was just black to them and they wouldn't accept me. When I tried to hang with the black kids things were fine until I started to speak. To them I was no longer black. I know the look in Amelia's judging eyes well. "You and I know that's bullshit. I never have understood you two. I figured you just didn't know how to satisfy him. He can be very insatiable and demanding," she purrs. I step closer to her. I can give two shits that she has at least five inches on me. I stand tall and crowd her space enough to let her know how serious I am.

"You sure you want to fuck with me, honey?" I tilt my head to the side. "There are reasons that *I* am his wife. You only get one warning and that's because I'm in the holiday spirit. Walk away, *puta.*"

"Vete al demonio," she hisses at me.

"I'll meet you there. I'm sure hell has a special place for a *zorra* like you that spends most of her time on her knees choking on other women's husband's *huveos.*"

She glares at me until something over my shoulder catches her attention. A smile comes to her botoxed face. This would be the one night I don't walk with my blades in my mouth.

Ugh! I'll still slap the shit out of her.

"You are nothing but a little street rat. He has already moved on. The way he always does," she says smugly.

She turns to slink away before I can put my paw print on her face. I roll my eyes, but Cristóbal's laughter from across the room draws my attention. Steam is already rolling off of me, before I dare to turn to see what I know is going to piss me off.

My husband is surrounded by women fawning all over him. Yet, it's the bleached blonde, tall Latina that sends fire through my veins. She's Cristóbal's usual type and she's leaning in laughing as if he's said the funniest thing in the world.

"Oh, he has me so fucked up," I say to myself and turn on my heels.

I hope that bitch smells my pussy on his breath, since she wants to be all up in his face. I saunter my ass right for the door. I fight over no man. I think of stopping to flirt with one of the men staring at me as I walk by, but I'm not even going to bother.

I showed my face. This trip is done. I pull my phone to order the jet ready for my flight to London.

"Where do you think you're going?"

I close my eyes as his voice washes over me. His heat meets my back, consuming me with his presence. I go to step away, but his large hand splays my belly.

"Don't ignore me, *Esposita*," he hisses next to my ear.

"You don't need me. You have plenty of women to give you attention," I say.

"But you are the only one I'm taking home to fuck," he says hotly.

"You wish."

A ripping sound greets my ears just before his front presses closer to my back. The heat from his body seeps into my skin, but I fight against sagging into him. I force the gasp back down my throat when his warm hand slide into my dress through opening he just made.

"I've been wanting to rip this dress from your body from the time I laid eyes on you coming down the stairs. Do you know how beautiful you are?" he says against my ear.

I go to snap at him but his tongue trailing the shell of my ear, stops me on a dime. I do moan and sag into him slightly. That ripping sound fills the air again as his palm reaches up higher beneath the fabric.

He turns me to face him so fast, I'm dazed when I look up at him. Those hazel-blue eyes blaze down at me. I've seen this look before.

It was the same look his gave me that night I stupidly fell into his bed. The night we consummated our marriage after eighteen years.

"Watch your head," he commands.

"What?" I ask before my feet leave the ground and I understand his intention.

He folds both our bodies into the waiting limo I hadn't even noticed appear. The door closes behind us as my back meets the bench seat.

Cristó tugs off his tux jacket, tossing it aside. He tears the rest of the side of my gown open, peeling the ruined dress from my body.

His eyes roam over me as he licks his lips. Goosebumps rise all over. I shiver, covering my breasts.

"Don't hide from me. I'm an old man, sí. You have nothing to fear," he says darkly.

I roll my eyes at him. "Cristó—"

"*Silencio.* You want to be rid of me. Give me my fill of this tight pussy and I'll let you go. I will give you your freedom," he says.

It shouldn't sting to hear him say those words. I turn away from him, not wanting him to see how much they do sting. Jealously tries to rear its head. In the past, I never allowed myself to think of his relationships and the women he would bed.

Now… I'd be lying if I said it hadn't boiled my blood every time my thoughts turned to him living his life here without me. I've had my heart broken enough. I won't lay my heart bare to Cristó.

Sex is sex. Giving him more time will change everything. It will leave my heart vulnerable. I know this for a fact. It's the reason why I ran a year ago.

"Ah," I gasp and whimper when his warm mouth wraps my nipple.

I turn back to find him watching me as he sucks on my breast. He pulls harder as his fingers slip beneath the fabric of my thong. He's making it impossible to ignore him.

My peak pops from his mouth. I watch the string of saliva that connects from my skin to his full lips. His fingers slip inside me and my back bows. I try to close my legs but his big body is wedged between my thighs as he kneels on the limo floor before me.

"Do your young lovers make you feel like this?" he says from between tight lips. "Do they make your pussy this wet?"

"Cristó," I cry out.

"*Sí, mi amor.* Do you call their names with such passion?"

I can't respond to his question. His thumb circling my clit is driving me crazy as he pumps his fingers in and out of me. Instead of telling him to fuck off, I pull my legs back and rock against his fingers.

Again, the sound of fabric tearing fills my ears. My thong is now nothing more than a scrap of material that Cristóbal tosses over his shoulder. His lips are on me before I can catch my breath.

He groans into me as he eats my pussy with purpose. I lock my fingers in the long strands at the top of his hair. It's not enough to anchor me. I don't know whether to grind against his face or push him away and run.

My hips have a mind of their own. Hot tears roll down my cheeks as he sends me into bliss. They are tears of overwhelming pleasure.

Only you, papi.

"Do they make you come this hard?" he pants as if speaking to my thoughts.

He doesn't give me time to answer as he thrusts into me. I didn't even see when he unfastened his pants. My legs wrap around his back, my hands go to his biceps. I grasp the tight muscles for dear life.

"Cristó, please," I cry.

"Do I fuck you like an old man? Do I feel like an old man to you?" he bites out.

"No, no, no," I whimper mindlessly.

"Do you want to be free of this cock, *mi amor*? Do you want me to stop fucking you?"

I bite my lip before I say something I'll regret. Hell no, he doesn't fuck like an old man. I can only dream of getting this kind of dick on a regular.

"*Coño*," I scream when he shifts my legs to his shoulders, lifts to his feet and starts to drill down into me.

My eyes drop to his abs flexing beneath his taut skin. My gaze drops further, pulling a moan from my lips as I watch his girth push in and out of me, covered in my juices. One of the sexiest sights I've ever seen, turning me on beyond belief.

He shoves his tongue into my mouth, stifling my screams. I can taste my essence all over his mouth. I begin to tremble and quiver beneath him. He breaks the kiss to give me an intense stare. Too intense for the way he's fucking me.

Feelings that have no business surfacing start to stir. It's too much, all of it. Multiples begin to rock my body and I gush all over him. I've never been fucked the way Cristóbal fucks me and I've had amazing sex before. This is some next level type of shit. My eyes widen in surprise when I feel him spill into me. I hadn't realized his didn't put on a condom. I go to protest and chide him, but he takes my lips in a hard demanding kiss.

"Forty-nine," his snorts against my lips. "I run ten miles every morning in the sand. Give me a better reason, *Esposita*."

He pulls from my body as the car comes to a stop. Quickly he dresses me in his tux jacket. My heavy lids threaten to close all on their own as he carries me from the car into the house.

"You are mine, Detra. This is why everything will change now," I hear him say before I fall asleep.

CHAPTER THREE

Taking Off

Detra

I groan as I wake, reaching out for the warm body that's been keeping me warm in my sleep. I suddenly feel the loss of the heat in my bones.

It's an odd feeling since I sleep alone most of the time. Yet, I can't shake it. I frown when I find cool sheets beside me. My brain starts to wake and I realize I'm reaching for Cristó and he's not there.

Opening my eyes, the clock comes into view. Five-fifteen it reads. I huff and turn over onto my back, pulling the covers up over my head. I can't believe he still went for his morning run.

"Seriously, aye," I huff.

I've been asleep for what… an hour max? He kept me up all night. Thankfully, over the past few days, he hasn't wasted any more time trying to convince me things need to change. At least, not with his words.

If you count the things he has done to my body that would be a different story. I swear the man has had a conversation with every inch of me from inside out. I furrow my brows and chew on my lips as I think about what those conversations said.

Something has changed between us. I can ignore it as much as I want, it's still there and it's screaming for me to admit it. I won't. I'm going to stay a few more days and then I'm headed to London to do my job, just like I always do.

My phone rings, pulling me from my wondering thoughts. I'm grateful and annoyed at the sometime. I'm on vacation, I shouldn't be getting calls and definitely not this early.

I didn't tell anyone where I was going but I'm only an hour ahead of New York's time zone. That makes it four in the morning there. Someone's trying to get their head taken off.

"Hello," I bite out.

"We have a problem. I'm calling you first because it's your boy," Manny's voice comes through the line.

I sit up and the sheet falls into my laps. I'm wide awake at the mention of my childhood best friend having a problem. Manny doesn't have to say his name for me to know he's talking about Nelson.

"What's going on?"

"He called in a car accident," he replies.

"Okay, his driver was drunk or something?" I ask in confusion.

"No, he was the driver. It was a few days ago, but he just called me. Apparently, the car was tampered with."

"What? When did this happen? Why is he calling you and not me?"

"Don't know. He sounded pissed and asked me to keep it quiet," he says.

"I don't want anyone touching that car until me and my boys get there. Sending my crew over. I'm on my way," I command as I toss off the covers and jump out of bed.

"I'm telling Cristóbal," he warns.

"What? Are we five?"

"Your friend is a major asset. It's enough you have me keeping the embezzlement from him," Manny huffs.

"I have that situation under control. Art isn't going to embarrass me in front of your brother. I've taken care of it."

"Yeah, but not the way Cristóbal or I would have," he says gruffly.

"Sometimes a gentler hand is needed. I learned that from Cristó himself," I retort.

There is a pause on the other end. I pull the phone from my ear to see if I've lost the connection. Placing it back, I get ready to say something when Manny's words cause me to freezes.

"Cristó?" His voice is laced with curiosity and humor. "Tell me, *amiga*, where are you?"

"I'm on my way to London," I say stiffly.

"From where?"

"I don't have to report to you."

"Tell *mi hermano* I said, hello," he roars with laughter.

I hang up on him. I'm not in the mood to get into this with Manny. He has asked me repeatedly why I chose to marry his brother. My answer has always been the same. It was the right thing to do for me.

I rub at my chest. I don't know if I'd give him the same answer if he asked me today. Which leads me to my husband. He's not going to be happy that I'm leaving so soon.

He mentioned plans for the New Year. I've never missed bringing in the New Year with Cristóbal. Not once since we've been married.

"Things are different," I tell myself as I start to feel guilty. I don't know what for. I'm free to come and go as I please. I'll come back in a few months just as we agreed. I'll just stay longer to make up for skipping a visit this year and for running off early this time.

"Yes, that will have to work. This is business. I've taken off to handle business before," I mutter.

So why are you rushing to leave before he returns?

I'll leave that question unanswered. I don't want to pay too much attention to why I pack my bag and run from my husband's home like I have a fire on my ass.

~B~

Cristóbal

From the moment I step into my home, I know something is off. I can feel it in my bones. It's as if the walls speak of the woman who is no longer here.

I roar with anger when I confirm she and her things are once again gone. I've had enough of this... this disrespect. It's time I remind my little wife that our marriage is not optional.

I pull out my phone and dial my brother. My teeth are clenched so tight they threaten to break. I'm ready to hit the roof when he doesn't answer on the first three rings.

"Hello, *hermano*," Manny says with a deep sigh when he finally answers.

"Where is she?"

"You two have taken things to a new level, I see," he says with humor in his voice.

"That is none of your business."

"I told you it was a matter of time. You've always secretly cared for her," he taunts. "*Sí*, you think she's smart and you wanted her and I to build a legacy since you've had it in your head you never want your own *niños*.

"But something else has been brewing in your thoughts for years. How do you think she will feel when she finds out you are the reason her old boyfriends always broke up with her when they got too close?"

"I will cut your tongue out if she ever finds out," I seethe. "Now tell me what I want to know."

"What makes you think I know? She didn't tell me she was going to Puerto Rico to spend time in your bed. Why would she tell where she plans to lie her head next?"

"My wife doesn't need to tell you when she's in my fucking bed. But it is your fucking job to know where the fuck she is when she's not with me," I snarl.

"Sí, just as I thought. You have slept with her," he chuckles.

"*Manny*," I drag out in warning, my accent thickening.

"She is on her way to London," he continues to chuckle.

"Why?"

"Nelson is there," he says more seriously. "We believe someone has tampered with his car. He had an accident of sorts. No one was harmed, but it was more than a flat tire as it would have initially appeared."

"*Carajo*," I say through clenched teeth. "What else are you not telling me?"

"You should have a talk with your *Teniente*. She has a lot you might want to listen to. That is if you have a conversation outside of your bed," he says.

"Where is Gabriella?" I ask, a smile coming to my lips.

"*Vete a la mierda*," he snaps.

"No thank you. You are not my type. Tell Gabby to meet me in London—"

"You will have to tell her yourself," he cuts me off.

"Are you losing control of the women, *mi hermano*?"

"I could ask you the same. Neither of them seem to be listening to you either."

"Gabriella and I have no issues," I scoff.

"Too bad you can't say the same for your wife," he clips out and hangs up.

I laugh as the line goes dead. I've given him a taste of his own medicine. My *Teniente* and *Sicarios* can be a handful. Yet, they are the best. My mind turns to my *esposa,* my *Teniente.* I don't regret making her my wife or second in command.

She just needs to remember who's first. I allowed Detra her freedom and that may have been my mistake, because now I'm finding that she's hiding things from me. I once thought Detra's father was the key to pulling the strings of her happiness.

I found out right after our marriage that this was not true at all. It's the funny looking best friend with the ideas. He is the one that my wife will move the earth for. He means as much to her as Manny does... or should I say, more.

I make another call as my mind is made up.

"Get the plane ready," I bite out, then hang up.

First a shower, then I pack. It is time I meet this Nelson Fisher. I want to know why she is so drawn to him and dedicated to his protection. It is more than keeping my investments secure.

I want to know how he makes you stay when I cannot.

CHAPTER FOUR

London Bridge

Detra

I expected Cristóbal to call me by now. I haven't heard a thing from him since I left. I shouldn't be this disappointed.

"You need anything else, cuz?"

I look up as my cousin, Emilio's, voice pulls me from my thoughts. I still can't focus as I stare at him. I can't stop thinking about Cristó and the weird place things have entered.

Hearing Nelson and Talina go at it hasn't helped me to keep my thoughts off of my husband either. I'll be honest, I wasn't ready to leave. I think that's the part that scares me most.

"Dee, yo, you all right?"

I focus on Emilio once again. My cousin is a straight New Yorker. Washington Heights all day. I used to love taking the train in from Jersey to hang with my family. Nelson would come along when his mom was too much to bear.

Washington Heights is what lead me to Cristó, it's where I met Manny. I always say Jersey made me grimy, but I got my street smarts and flavor from the Heights. I smile at the memories. That was before. Before my father let his other life spill over and I had to put my street smarts to use.

"I'm good. Just get that to the lab and let me know what you find. Send it all to Manny too. Hopefully they didn't screw up any clues that will help us," I reply.

"What does Nelson want us to do with the whip?"

"Chop it. I already ordered him a new one." I shrug.

Emilio shakes his head. "Chop it, she says. Like it's a fucking Honda or something. I need a promotion," he mutters, sucking his teeth.

"I would have given you one, but you don't want to go to school for the positions I've offered you," I toss back.

"You bugging. I'm not cut out for that. You like all that reading and studying and shit. These streets are what I study, Ma."

"Which is why you're not getting promoted. What part of the streets you studied got you to London, Papa? I'll wait…" I pause to allow him to answer.

"True, but you don't have to say it like that," he says twisting his lips.

I grin at my cousin. It's not like I don't pay him well. He loves to tease that I don't pay him enough for the things he does for me, when that's far from the case.

"Did you check your bank account this morning?"

He beams at me. Like I said, I take care of my family. They keep things running. Manny and I wouldn't be able to run things without them.

"Yeah, thanks. That was a nice Christmas gift," he chuckles.

"*De nada.* I appreciate you coming out here. I know you had plans."

"There's plenty of T and A here in London. I'm going to hit a few spots as soon as I get this work wrapped up. You think your boy Nelson wants to go out?"

"Ha! Nelson will not be making an appearance for a while. Cuba, Raj, and the rest of the crew are flying in this evening. You'll have company," I laugh.

"What? You too good to hang out with us now?" he teases.

"No." My smile falters. "I have work to do."

It's a lie and the truth. While I do need to find out who's behind tampering with Nelson's car, I'm also not in the mood to party. Funny, I never thought of my partying days as being behind me.

I'm thirty-eight, but I've kept up a decent social life. Nelson and I have afforded ourselves the finest when it comes to invites and hot spots with unlimited access. I'm just not in the mood to be social. I have too much on my mind.

I see the look in Emilio's eyes and know he's getting ready to pry. Some of my family knows I work for the big boss. Those that do, don't need to know I'm his wife or that I sleep with him.

The truth is, I'm glad none of my blood family has ever had an interest in moving up too high in the Suarez family ranks. On the surface you see Fisher, Inc., the marketing corporation. Some know there's more to it, others not so much.

I like to keep it that way. There are rules and levels to this. I breathe a sigh of relief when my phone rings cutting off Emilio's chance. I turn to walk away as I answer the call.

"*Hola.*"

"You're not going to like this," Gabriella says into the phone.

"I'll call you back in five," I rush out.

I need a secure line and some place private. Something tells me things are about to start falling down around me. Gabriella never calls me, I call her.

What fresh hell comes for my door? Coño!

~B~

Cristóbal

I will not ask my wife what she's been hiding from me. I'll find out my damn self. The more I think about it the more it pisses me off. Manny has known all of this and said nothing.

Have I fallen weak in my old age?

Screams pull me from my musing. I look at the sweaty piece of shit in front of me. He has fallen to his knees with his head bent, panting. Wiping the bloody knife in my hand on my shirt, I squat before him.

Placing the tip of the knife beneath his chin, I lift his head looking into his thieving eyes. Fear radiates from him as it should. He thought he was stealing from Nelson Fisher, but I'm the bank behind Fisher, Inc. That's my money.

"Art? This is your name," I ask tilting my head. I already know the answer.

"Y-yes," he whimpers.

"You steal from me, sí? Do you still think this was a wise thing?"

"I… I… I didn't know. I… I didn't steal from you," he stutters.

"You know, as a boy I spent a lot of time in New York. The fast pace caused me to have a quick mind," I tap my temple with my free hand. "I learned how to spot a rat, thief, and trader. You reek of all of those.

"You are also a liar. You lie to my face," I take my knife and slash it across his lying mouth.

More screams fill the air. It has been years since I've gotten my hands dirty, but I've always gotten into my work when I've had to. This is no different.

"I should be on my way to see my wife, but I've had to make a detour for you. She was too lenient on you. I do not possess this type of," I wave my knife in the air searching for the word. "Ah, mercy."

"Please," he tries to cry around his slit mouth.

"Tell me who helped you. If you do, I may find it in my heart to allow you *misericordia*," I say with a smile.

He shakes his head. Denying my request. He's protecting someone. It's going to cost him more pain than it's worth, I'm sure.

"I… it was just m… me," his slurs and gurgles.

Blood pours from his face. I grow tired of this. I stand looking around the old cemetery. Without a thought, I kick Art back into the open grave that was freshly dug for him.

"She's not going to like that you did this. She had a plan for him," Manny says.

"*She's* not going to like? *She's* not going to like?" My voice raises with each word. "*I* don't like you keeping things from me. *I* don't like that he was allowed to steal from me for so long."

"You asked her to keep your money clean. You have told her to keep her own hands clean. She handled it the best way she could while doing what *you* told her," he seethes back.

"Maybe it's time I give her job to someone else," I say.

"Someone sloppy that will land us all in jail? Someone as reckless as you used to be? Come on, *hermano*, think with *tu cabeza.*"

"Careful, *mi hermano*. You and I have much to talk about. You are my eyes and ears, but you have not been watching and listening for me," I warn.

"*Sí*, I have. I've watched over what's most important to you even before you were willing to admit it to yourself," he bellows, chest heaving. "I've done everything you've asked of me. Even when it hurts. Even when this is not what I want."

I close my eyes. I can feel and taste his pain. I know it well. I was wrong in the past to tell him to think of the family first. I know that now.

"*Sí*, this is a problem. One I plan to fix. There will be no more of this. I was young and I made mistakes—"

"You did what you thought was best. We all made our own mistakes. Go to your wife. You two were made for each other," he says, rubbing his forehead.

I grunt and turn to leave. My head filled with new thoughts and questions. I've done everything the way I thought my father wouldn't. I did everything to keep from landing in prison, alone, and eventually murdered.

"Cristóbal," I stop and turn. "I want you to meet my son."

My brows pinch. Manny sighs and runs a hand through the front of his hair. His brows knot mirroring mine.

"He's going to be one. We didn't—"

I hold up a hand. "*Hermano*, let's go to your place and have a long chat. It seems we have lost touch somewhere."

He nods tightly. I draw in a breath and wave my little brother over. My anger weans. I pat his chest.

"Never keep things from me again," I say.

"To be honest, I didn't know," he huffs.

"Oh, this keeps getting interesting."

CHAPTER FIVE

You Need Me

Detra

I lift a brow at the reflection of the hairstylist in the mirror. I needed to get out of the house before Nelson and Talina drove me insane. However, this heifer is about to make me cut her.

My hair is a mix of my Mommy and Papi. Curly, but not the silky texture of my dad's. The way this wench is looking at it, you'd think it was a mop that smelled. All I want is a wash and set.

I needed my scalp massaged to hopefully rub the sounds of Nelson breaking Talina's back out of my head. Sounds that have me longing for my husband. The man has rendered my vibrator useless. The thing feels more like a tickle after what Cristóbal has done to my body.

Ugh, here you go again.

I thought I had a hard time pushing Cristó out of my mind the first time. This last visit has been weighing my thoughts down and keeping me up at night. It's so powerful that even an hour later, after having my hair washed and set, my thoughts are still on him.

As I sit with my eyes closed I swear I can smell him. This chick clucks her tongue as she combs through my curls and I have to bite my tongue not to throat punch her. Her attitude hasn't changed a bit.

Between this hairdresser's attitude and my insistent thoughts about my husband, I'm ready to rip her a new one. The comb stops moving through my hair and I feel her shift away from me. A much larger hand runs through my scalp, causing goosebumps to cover my skin.

I gasp, not wanting to open my eyes. The scent of his cologne is too strong for me to be imagining things. The hand runs through the backside of my hair pushing it away from my neck.

I open my eyes just in time to see Cristóbal plant a kiss— that sends lightning bolts through my entire being—on the side of my throat. Damn this man. Those hazel-blue eyes capture my gaze and hold it. The heat I see in them causes my pulse to race.

"What are you doing here?"

"Is that anyway to greet your husband, *Esposita?*" he says against my skin, his beard tickling me.

I shiver and ball my fists. Our eyes remain on each other's as he lifts to his full height. The electric blue suit and grey shirt draping his body scream power and suave.

He reaches into his suit jacket and retrieves his wallet. Pulling a few notes, he waves that stylist over. She scurries closer.

"She's done here," he says.

"Don't tip that bitch."

He chuckles at me, piling off a few notes. I narrow my eyes at him, but it's useless. He has my elbow in one hand and my purse in the other. I'm on my feet as he leads me out of the salon.

"Cristó, what the hell?" I hiss as my little legs try to keep up with his quick pace.

"You wasted your time getting your hair done. I'm going to fuck it into a mess," he breathes into my ear.

"Are you crazy? You can't just show up demanding sex," I say as he starts to shove me into the back of his waiting car.

He slides in after me, tossing my things aside. When he levels me with a glare, I almost have a mind to shrink back. I've never cowed to anyone, but the sexy, crazy look in his eyes makes me second-guess that one.

"If you think I'm here to just demand sex, I might have to rethink the credit I give you," he says. "First, I'm going to fuck you until you can't walk for leaving my bed, my home and not telling me. Then, I'm going to find out why you felt you needed to cut our time short to be here, from your lips.

"I warn you, *pequeño*. Don't lie to me. I've been looking into what you've been up to behind my back. I know *everything*."

"What do you think you know?" I toss back.

"This *cabrón*, Art," he says and watches as my face tightens. "*Sí*, I thought you would know that name. I don't like you keeping things from me."

"I had it handled," I grumble.

"No," he barks. "I have handled it. You... you have patted this problem on the hand. You are stronger than that. I've taught you better."

"Are you questioning my judgement?" I seethe. "I had reasons for handling things the way I have. You think I don't know you have been digging into *my* problems? I'm getting phone calls about you prying into things that don't concern you.

"I don't need you to come stomping all over what you *feel* I have not handled right. Fuck, Cristó. I can't believe you just took a shit in my backyard without telling me."

"*Your* backyard?" He lifts a brow. "I think you are forgetting who this all belongs to."

I push closer to him to get into his face. "I haven't forgotten a thing. I think you are forgetting who to trust. Stop thinking with your dick and think with your head."

Wrong move. He has a hand in my hair, tugging my head back before I can process the move. His eyes are hard and all signs of the friend and husband I've come to know are gone. In their place is the man that has built an empire even before I showed up on his doorstep.

"Watch who you are talking to, Detra. I've been doing this before you knew how to wipe your pussy, let alone bring a man to his knees with it. I made the call you should have.

"I took care of your little problem without leaving a trail. Don't over play your position with me. I will always be on top. You just make sure you don't lose your value to me," he says with deathly calm.

"Does that mean in your bed or in your family?" I say defiantly.

"Watch it, *corazón*," he says tightly.

"Don't threaten me, Cristó."

"Why do I bother?" he huffs before crushing my mouth with his.

He devours my mouth, dousing my fire. My fingers are locked in his hair before I can refrain from falling into his spell. He's panting as hard as I am as he consumes me.

His hands and mouth manipulate me into his demands. I'm pressed against him needing something I don't want to need and wanting everything I shouldn't want. When he lets me up for air, I can't even remember why I was supposed be so pissed off at him.

"You will learn I always win, *Esposita*," he breathes against my lips.

"*Vamos a ver*," I toss back.

"Sí, we will see."

~B~

Cristóbal

I look over my shoulder at my naked sleeping wife. My eyes travel her body lazily taking her in. When I land on her hair my lips twitch into a smile.

It's a sweaty mess. Just the way I wanted. I can get used to this makeup sex.

But did we make up?

I scrub a hand down my beard. I don't think we have. She is so independent and that's the way I want her. It's the way I've always known her to be, but I don't like this idea of her challenging me.

The problem is, I don't think it's the challenge in business that bothers me most. My bed is where she belongs. I just need to figure out how to keep her here.

Frowning, I turn away and stand from the bed. Sitting here isn't going to solve anything for anyone. I walk out into the common area, slipping into a robe.

Collecting my phone from the trail of clothing we left behind, I dial the last missed call and place the phone to my ear. My gaze falls on Detra's torn dress and a smile comes to my lips.

As good as she looked in the black sheath, I enjoyed tearing it from her body more.

"*Hola, Jefe*. I have that information you asked for," Alonso answers the line, pulling my attention from thoughts of my wife.

"Good, bring it to my room. Also, make dinner reservations. Someplace special. Call in a few favors," I command.

There is a moment's hesitation before Alonso replies. "For two?"

"Why do you ask me such stupid questions? *Sí*, for two. Did I not come here for my wife?"

"*Sí, sí*, I just wanted to check, *Jefe*," he rushes out.

I narrow my eyes as if he were in front of me. *Sí*, I have many changes I will be making. First, I will deal with my wife. Then, I'll handle those that think I don't see them.

"Alonso?"

"*Sí, Jefe.*"

"Loyalty is everything in this life. I'm grateful for those that have remained so loyal to me. It does not go unnoticed," I say.

"*Gracias, Jefe.*"

I hang up. Wise men hear what is said. Entitled men hear what they want. I have survived many by becoming the former.

CHAPTER SIX

Dinner

Detra

I'm not going to let this man keep ripping up my clothes. I see the way he's eyeing this dress. I don't care if he bought it. I like it and the one still in tatters on his hotel room floor.

"Why are you here?" I ask for the hundredth time.

"You are beginning to wound my pride. From the way you were screaming my name this afternoon, I thought you were happy to see me. No?" he replies.

"That's not an answer to my question and you know it."

"I don't like this question. You are my wife. You should be wherever I am," he says tightly.

My grip tightens on my fork. My belly shouldn't flip every time he calls me his wife. I hate that my nipples are so hard they are chaffing against the fabric of my bra.

"But you were not here. You are now and I want to know why," I reply.

"You're problem is that you can't help that smartass mouth of yours," he says glaring at me. "When are you going to realize that I am not going anywhere. You will have to face me."

I tilt my head to the side, studying my husband. I think I know Cristóbal better than anyone. I know him well enough to know that he has locked in on this mission to make more of what we are to each other.

That's not good for me.

"What if I don't want to face," I wave my fork between the two of us, "this?"

He mirrors my body language, tilting his head to the opposite side. Something about the move makes me feel like prey. I straighten in my seat, prepared to protect myself.

"You will face *us*," he says. "You have no choice."

"I always have a choice, darling. You are the one that taught me that," I purr at him.

"*Sí*, I did teach you this. But you have also learned that I always get what I want. I've taught you to do the same, and no matter how much you want to deny it, you want this as much as I do."

"No, I—"

"Don't. We don't lie to each other. Don't give me this bullshit. You are scared. I just have not figured out of what," he says cutting my words off.

I bristle at this. It's hit the mark, but that doesn't mean I like it. I turn away from him, not wanting him to see the truth in my eyes.

"I like my freedom."

"*Sí*, you do. I will not take this from you."

"Come on, Cristó. That's a lie. I'm not moving to Puerto Rico. I have a life."

He falls back in his seat, his lips pinched. "You mean, you have Nelson," he says with a glare.

I grin at him. My husband is showing a new side of himself. A side I never thought I'd see on Cristóbal Suarez.

"Are you jealous, *Marido?*"

"Mmm," he releases the sound as if I've just sucked him into my mouth. "You are finally admitting that I'm your husband. This is a start."

"I have never denied that you are my husband. I just liked it better when you were my silent husband."

"You say the words, but your body betrays you even now," he replies leaning into the table. "I don't have to make noises when I'm eating your pussy. I just know you like it."

I have to catch myself from drooling. It's no wonder his bed has never been empty. With a mouth like that and the skills he puts down, no woman in her right mind would deny him.

"We need more than sex for a real marriage," I murmur, not able to meet his gaze.

"And we have had that for the last nineteen years. We've been building our friendship, no? We of all people in the world have what it takes to be in a real marriage," he counters.

"What if I want children?" I ask, feeling a victory in my grasp.

"Then, we will enjoy making them. You are thirty-eight. Still plenty of time for us to have a family. You will give me gorgeous children," he says with a devilish smile on his full lips.

"Aren't you too old to be thinking of children?"

"Do I have to remind you of what happened the last time you called me old?" he taunts, pinning me with a pointed look.

"This is ridiculous."

"That I want to have children with my wife?"

My confidence deflates. He's serious. I see it in his eyes. He never used to want children.

"What the hell has happened to you? You have always been adamant that you don't want children. Why now?"

"Because you have asked for them. Because it would be with you," he says smoothly.

My fork and plate forgotten, I palm my face and blow out a breath. I don't want a real marriage. I don't want love. Love ruined my life. Love made me the hard woman I am. Love brought me to Cristóbal's door.

My family doesn't do right by love. We just don't do well with that word at all. I blame my dad. He taught us all that love hurts.

"I don't want this change," I whisper.

"*Esposita*—"

"No," I shake my head.

"Detra, listen me. *Mira, mira*," he says firmly, but gently when I won't look at him. I lift my eyes to his slowly. "I have—"

"Cristóbal? Is that you?" a woman's voice sings.

I watch my husband tense. Not liking the look on his face, I turn to find the owner of the voice. Of course, another big tittie, blonde.

I purse my lips and roll my jaw. This is why I'm not falling into this trap. One day he's going to wake up and the lure of my young pussy will wear off. He will be back to bedding big breasted, pale skinned Latinas.

I'm not his type, she is. Why play myself? I'm going to finish here in London and go back to New York to lick my wounds.

I slam shut the door I came so close to pulling open. I return to my meal as if neither of them exist. At least, I try. My poor chicken and veggies are getting stabbed to death in my efforts.

~B~

Cristóbal

That voice makes my skin itch. Of all the places, of all the moments, this is not the one for this woman to appear. My life is starting to fill with regrets.

I watched as Detra had been about to cave. I'd been so close to reaching her. Now, I can see her closing off from me again.

"You've gotten more handsome with time, *amante*," she purrs.

"I have not been your lover for years. Don't disrespect my wife addressing me as such," I seethe.

"Your wife?" she squawks. "I've heard rumors say that—"

"Do I look like I care about rumors. You see her seated here. I've just told you who she is," I say and glare.

"*Sí, sí,* I apologize. Have a good evening, Señor Suarez."

I stare at Detra as she stabs at her food. Releasing a sigh, I signal for the check. I know better than to provoke a scorpion. This will need to pass.

But God is she beautiful when she's angry.

CHAPTER SEVEN

Divorce

Detra

"Come take a shower with me," he says in my ear as he steps behind me and begins to lower my zipper.

I glare at him through our reflection in the mirror, while I remove my earrings. I scowl harder when I glance at the topknot in my hair. He made good on his word earlier, ruining my freshly washed and set do.

"I'm not in the mood," I say, ignoring his bare torso.

He kisses my neck and shoulder. "I can fix that, *cariño.*"

"No you cannot."

I pull away from him and move to the other side of the room. I fumble to get my clutch open. I need my phone. I'll be leaving to return to Nelson's place. I will not spend the night here.

The only way I'll get my husband out of my system is to stop letting him put his hands on me. I will be the one to end this, since he seems to forget this was not the plan. If he wants change, I have some change for him.

"I want a divorce," I say as I feel his eyes on me.

I don't look up from texting for a ride to come for me. I don't care to see his reaction. I just want to be done.

"You know that has never been an option," he says so coolly, I do lift my head.

"Why not?"

"Are you forgetting who you are?"

"Watch your tone with me," I warn him.

He is across the room in a few short steps. I lift my chin and throw my shoulders back, meeting him head on. I will not shrink back from him.

"*You* are telling *me* to watch *my* tone with *you*? *Sí*, you have not only forgotten who you are, you have forgotten who I am. There will be no divorce.

"You belong to me. In and out of my bed. You are mine. There will be no walking away from me," he says icily.

"I can do my job and not be married to you," I demand.

"Funny, but isn't that the reason we married? Because you could not."

My nostrils flare. His chilly words hit their mark. He is right, but things have changed since I was that young girl, desperate to find a way to fix things.

I take another approach. "Why keep me around? You don't trust my judgement. You have decided to do my job for me."

"You are trying me. It is not a wise thing."

"Why not? Do you plan to take care of me too," I taunt.

Something shifts in his eyes and I know I've gone too far. Heat fuses with ice. There's danger in his gaze that I'm not sure I can save myself from.

I take a step back. "Don't," I warn.

"*Sí*," he says huskily, before grasping my waist and tugging me forward.

~B~

Cristóbal

"I said, don't," she repeats, even as her body sags into mine. "You do not mean this. In fact, I think you like provoking me. Divorce," I scoff, moving my hands to her ass. "We will never divorce. You have played with your little toys.

"Why are you so angry to see one of mine? It's not as if you didn't know they exist."

"First, I could care less about the disrespectful *putas* you spend your time fucking. You will give me a divorce," she replies.

I lift her from her feet and pull her legs around my waist. Her eyes grow wide and her hands wrap my neck. The more she challenges me the harder I get.

"Look into my eyes and tell me you do not feel this between us. Tell me I don't consume your thoughts, *mi amor*."

She shivers in my hold, her eyes squeezing shut. I see the change that happens against her protests. She softens in my arms.

"Stop," she pleas. "Whatever this is. Just stop."

I peck her lips. "Why should we?" I kiss her nose. "Why would we?" I lick from her throat up to her lips, nipping her full bottom one. "Even if we could, why? *Mi amor*, I didn't know what I had all of this time. I don't want to stop now."

"Cristó?"

"*Sí, mi amor?*"

Slipping my hand beneath her dress and into her panties, I begin to play with her pussy from behind. She's already soaked. I groan, wanting inside of her now, but knowing I'm going to take my time.

Pulling the zipper the rest of the way down, I lift the dress up and tug it over her head. Her breasts jiggle free, bare and begging for my attention.

"Please?" she pleads.

"Please what, *corazón*?" I whisper against her collarbone.

"Cristó," she says, a plea and warning in her voice.

I chuckle darkly. I know what she needs, but first we need to get a few things clear. I slip my fingers from her hot core and bring them to my lips.

Her eyes glaze with lust as I suck her flavor from my digits. She tastes so good on my tongue. I can't wait to devour her whole.

Keeping my eyes on hers, I drag my wet fingers over her lips. She parts them for me and pulls the wet offering in. My jaw works and my cock twitches demanding release as she licks my fingers clean.

"I will give you what you need, but first, we settle our little problem. I want you. I will not rest until I have you in every way. You are not some toy I want to play with and throw away. You know me, *mi amor*. You know the core of me," I say.

Her lips tremble and it's the most vulnerable I've ever seen her. It makes me weak in the knees. She's allowing me to see something no one else will ever see.

Don't forget about Nelson.

Ah, sí. The friend. The one she always goes running to. Still, I know in my heart this is a level of intimacy that only I will have with my wife.

"I can't give you what you want," she says softly.

"Stop defying me just because you feel you should or you think you can. Give yourself to me."

"Stop pushing me when you know I can't."

"You can and you will," I say before crushing her lips.

The kiss is so rough and all-consuming, I taste the tinge of blood on our tongues. She doesn't tear away from me though. Teeth, tongues, and lips still continue to collide.

"You drive me *loco*," I groan. "I'm going to make love to you until neither of us can breathe."

"Cristó," she whimpers.

"I love when you call my name, *mi amor*," I say, pulling a shiver from her body.

I twist my fist in the thin fabric of her panties and tear them free from her body. She drops her forehead to my chin, an act of her surrender. I run my fingers up and down her spine, teasing.

"This means nothing," she whispers.

I frown and still. I will make her swallow those words. We have always meant something to each other. Hours upon hours together when she came to me. I've shared things with her I've never shared with anyone else.

There will never be a time when we mean nothing. Everything between us means something. *Everything.*

I shift her body up my torso to reach my pants. I'd already removed everything else to take my shower. I make quick work of removing my pants and boxer briefs.

Detra grinds against my cock as soon as it's free and pointing up at her. She's slick and ready for me. I would torture her if I didn't need her so badly.

All thoughts of taking my time vanish when she sucks on my neck. She's a wicked woman, who has more control over me than she knows.

"Ah," she cries out as I thrust up into her.

"I have not even begun," I say through tight lips.

Grasping her waist, I stop to move her body up and down on my length. Her heat traps me in her warm walls with each thrust. She's so wet, I can feel her dipping down my thighs.

Her cries fill the room, but it's not enough. I want to nail the thought of *nothing* out of her head. She means everything to me.

"Look at me," I demand.

She lifts her head from my neck. I reach beneath both of her thighs, cradling her body and supporting her weight on my forearms. My hands lock together at the center of her back and I start to bounce her on my cock.

Her eyes bulge and she starts to scream in pleasure. Her head tosses back, her breasts jiggle with the force of me bouncing her. She's becoming slicker with each up and down motion.

"This… this means nothing? You tell me that now," I grind out.

"Oh my God!"

"No, I'm your husband."

"Fuck, Cristó. Please, I can't. Fuck," she whimpers and gasps.

"You still want a divorce? Your pussy says you are happy right where you are, *Esposita*," I taunt as she soaks my balls and thighs.

"That's not fair," she bites out half-heartedly.

"What's not fair, *mi amor*?" I breathe. "I can tell you many things that are not fair."

"You're not right, my chest, shit. I'm coming," she screams, eyes rolling back.

~B~

Detra

He is so wrong for this. This is exactly way I never should have opened this door. Who fucks someone's brains out like this? I'm serious. My heart is pounding and feels like it's going to burst free from my chest.

I'm so wet, if he weren't in complete control of my body and his, I think he would have slipped out by now. Damn, this shit just isn't right. A divorce? I want to marry his dick game.

He places his lips to my ear. "You know what's not fair. You making me wait an entire year to get back into this pussy. My pussy," he says huskily, licking my ear.

"I've been waiting, giving you time to come to me. Not fair, is waking up to find my wife gone. Not fair is going for a run to again not find you in my bed.

"We mean something, we mean more than the shit you keep pulling with me. Don't ever tell me my touch on your body will mean nothing. As long as my blood and soul burn for you, we will always mean something," he grunts out.

I shatter again. It feels like my belly drops out. I'm limp in his hold. Kissing my temple he has mercy on me and stops driving into me as he bounces my body. I close my eyes as my back hits the cool bedspread.

However, sleep is not what greets me. Cristó doesn't pull out. Instead, he starts to slow grind. I bite my lip to keep from crying out. His lips latch onto my neck and he begins to suck.

I open my eyes, my lids fluttering as I look up at the ceiling. The brush and stroke of his beard sends too many sensations running through me. My nipples are rock hard and my thighs tremble, warning that the rest of my body is about to convulse.

He starts to grunt and groan as his big body grinds and rolls into mine. The vibration from his moaning against my neck pulls the trigger I need to go over. This man is a wrecking ball to my body.

"You will only come for me. No man will ever touch you. You're my wife. You will always be my wife," he moans. "*Mierda*, come for me one more time. I want you with me."

"Coño, I'm going to have a heart attack," I cry.

He shifts to lick over the center of my chest. He makes a trail of kisses to my right breast and wraps his heated mouth around my tightened peak.

"Cristó."

Calling his name is like igniting a fire. He looks up at me with those hazel-blue eyes and starts to pound into me. The glare in his eyes says so much. He's staking a claim, putting me in my place, and dominating my body all at once.

My breast pops free from his mouth and he bears his teeth. I reach to cup his face, burying my fingers into his beard. He moves up my body again and crushes my lips.

The kiss is hard and hot, just like earlier. I'm deliriously close to telling him I'll stay with him forever. I don't even remember why we were fighting.

"Let me in, *novia*," he says with so much passion. "Let me all the way in."

I turn away from his eyes, but he moves his lips to my ear and continues to rumble pleas for my submission. I would surrender if it weren't my heart on the line, but I can't. My life was shaped by the things love makes people do.

"Your heart speaks as loudly as your body. Our sex reeks of passion beyond friendship or a simple fuck. For now, I will give you pleasure…."

His words trail off and I'm too shaken to my core to pry into where they were headed. I squeeze my eyes shut as I explode around him. I try to ignore the way his words burn through my heart. I try, doesn't mean I succeed.

Might want to second-guess that divorce though.

CHAPTER EIGHT

Alarm

Detra

My phone won't stop buzzing, but I'm too spent to answer it. I just want to sleep for the next week. I have no idea where his old ass gets all of that damn energy.

If I would have come one more time, I would have been in a coma. I groan into my pillow and wiggle my sore ass beneath the sheets. The insistent buzzing won't stop.

I'm going to kill whoever is on the other end. When the phone stops and starts again, I know I have to answer. However, before I can, my husband reaches across my back and grabs the phone from the nightstand.

"Hello," his deep voice croons as if he's already started his day. "This is Detra's phone. You are speaking to her husband. How can I help you?"

He pauses to listen and I pop up to take the phone from him. He could be talking to anyone. Including my father or mother that knows nothing about him.

My heart starts to race. I don't want my family to find out about him this way. My mother would kill me.

"I am a partner in the company. You can say what you need to say to me," he grinds out.

I pluck the phone from his hand, but he places it on speaker with his long fingers. I purse my lips at him. However, I allow him to listen in on the call.

"What's going on?" I say, looking to see that it's my office assistant.

"There has been a break in Ms. Marques," she replies.

Cristóbal glares at me. I've never used my married name in the office. I shrug my shoulders at him.

"Has anything been taken?" I ask, directing my attention back to the call.

"It looks as if they were trying to enter Mr. Fisher's office. You told me to call you directly if something like this ever happened," she replies.

"You did the right thing. I'm on my way," I say and end the call.

"We are going to New York?"

"*I* am going to New York," I say, dragging my stiff body from the bed.

"*Sí*, we are going to New York."

"Your Spanish is starting to sound like French and I don't like it."

"I don't like a lot of things, but I will wait until we are on our flight before I start to list them," he grumbles getting out of bed.

I ignore him as I try to walk on my wobbly legs. They threaten to buckle on me at any given moment. I would love a bath and time to soak, but that's not going to happen.

First, Nelson's car, now this. I'm going to get to the bottom of this sooner rather than later and someone is going to be sorry. If Cristó handled Art, that rules him out. Initially, he was at the top of my list. I was sure he had tried to pull some strings and have some reach.

Now, I'm a bit stunned and hungry for answers. I can't have Cristóbal truly thinking I have gone weak. I've done things differently in the last few years, but I've not lost my edge.

"I have called for my jet. A car is waiting downstairs," Cristó says as I pull the clothes from the bag he had delivered yesterday after destroying my dress.

"I could have called for my own plane and ride."

"You refuse the armored cars," he replies.

"Not my style. I prefer the cars I choose."

"It all belongs to me," he says gruffly.

"I will buy you out whenever you're ready," I challenge, reminding him that I have built assets beyond him.

"Let's go. You are wasting time," he grunts and walks out of the room.

~B~

Cristóbal

She may not want my help, but she has no choice. I do not like the events that have been taking place. Detra has yet to inform me of it all herself.

My patience grows thin, but not with her. The report I received was far from satisfactory. This is why I'm making this trip with her.

Not because I think she cannot handle things. I'm going to see everything with my own eyes. I also made a small connection with my wife last night that I don't want to break.

"Should I stay here in London? Do you think you will return here?" Alonso asks.

"Stay here and get me what I've been asking for. I want answers. Not this empty fluff you've given me," I say into the phone.

"I'm sorry. It was the best I could do on short notice."

"*Silencio*, I will not have these excuses. Remember, if I have to do your job, I don't need you. I want to know about this crash and the break in. Find out more about this Nelson. More than what you have been feeding me over the years. I want to know everything," I bark.

"Yes, *Jefe*. I will handle it," he mumbles.

"I know you will. Have it all for me by the time I land."

CHAPTER NINE

Little Sister

Detra

"They didn't get into your office, but they damn sure tried," I say into the phone as I rub my temples.

"I don't believe in coincidences," Nelson replies.

"I know you don't. Neither do I. I just need to figure out who could get to your car and try to get into your office."

"I'll come back."

"No, that's not necessary. Leave this me to." I sigh.

"I think we should let Brenda go. She and Art worked together for years. I just would rather cut ties," Nelson muses.

"That makes sense," I rub the back of my neck. "Listen, let me tie some things up here and I'll give you an update later. I'll take care of this."

"Be safe," he says.

"Always."

I end the call and turn to walk back to my office where I left Cristóbal. He insisted on coming with me to check on things. I would much rather he find a hotel to stay in or go to his brother's.

Anywhere that will ensure me he will not run into any of my family. I need to focus, but that's hard to do with my husband here in New York. All it takes is one family member and I'm fucked.

My family will descend like wolves. Thank God my place is here in New York and not Jersey. I can't even begin to count how many times that toll has kept my cheap ass family out of my hair. I like it that way.

"Andrea?" I call as the little weird chick appears in front of me.

This girl is one odd duck if I've ever seen one. My brain starts to work. She's supposed to be on vacation. She made the request after the auction.

What everyone around here doesn't know is that I know every single detail about this company. Everyone reports to me. Human Resources ran her time by me before it was approved.

"Hello, happy holidays," she says while bouncing on her toes and giving me a geeky smile.

I narrow my eyes on her little weird ass. There is just something I can't put my finger on. I go to ask her what the hell she's doing here, but my husband and my sister pick this exact moment to head in my direction.

Neither of them can see me from their angle. Nor can they see each other moving through the corridor.

"You, let's go," I command, grabbing Andrea's arm and dragging her with me.

Walking quickly, I head for the back hallway that will lead back around to the elevators. Andrea's goofy ass trips a few times, but I just tug her along with me.

If I dip out now, I can dodge them both. I freeze halfway to the elevator and groan. This was a bad idea. I panicked.

That man has jacked my head up and I haven't been thinking straight. If Jada asks Cristó who he is, he's going to say he's my husband.

"Shit, shit, shit," I huff and stomp my foot.

"Everything okay?" Andrea asks pushing up her glasses.

"I need to stop that train wreck I just left behind, but I want to know why you are here?" I demand.

"Penny called all of the junior assistants in. I just got turned around. They're down two levels in the cafeteria," she says awkwardly.

I shoot my assistant Penny a message to double check. She replies immediately calling Andrea a nitwit. Releasing her, I nod for the elevators.

"They're waiting for you," I say and turn back for my fate.

A chill runs through me as I move as fast as my feet will carry me. I'm tempted to kick off my heels and make a run for it. I have this ache in my stomach that tells me I'm too damn late.

When I hit the corner and hear my sister's voice, all the blood drains from my face. I skid to a halt and close my eyes. I'm so fucked. I run through the list of all of my private properties, wondering which one I can get to and leave all this behind.

Shit, Nelson. I'm more loyal to you than my own family.

Nelson is the only reason I don't turn and run from all of this and start a new life. What my husband doesn't know is that although I respect him, I trust no one in this life.

I've been securing my exit route for years. I could leave all of this behind. I have the plastic surgeon to make it all happen on speed dial.

"Listen, you're going to tell me who you are or I'm going to cut your ass up right where you stand, old man," Jada hisses in that mix of New York, Jersey, Latina all of my sisters have grown up with and still have.

I groan. Carrying blades in our mouths is also a family trait, Jada also walks with a switch blade. You can take the girls out of the hood, but never the hood out of the girls.

Coño.

~B~

Cristóbal

If I hadn't already seen pictures of my wife's siblings when I dug into her background, I still would have no question whether or not this little, spicy chica is related to my *Esposita*. She has the same eyes, same brown skin, and the same full, foul mouth. Their family is full of gorgeous women.

I can't help but wonder what my daughters will look like. Will they have their mother and *tía's* cute nose, will they make the same cute face in anger. I'm so lost in the amusement of my thoughts, I don't hear a thing she says until she threatens to cut me.

Knowing how fast my wife is to pull a blade from her mouth and slice someone open, I give this tiny one before me my full attention. I will not allow my thoughts to cause me to have to warm someone my wife cares for.

"Old man. Those words are starting to get on my nerves," I scoff and mumble to myself. "I am Cristóbal."

"*I am Cristóbal,*" she mocks, saying it through her nose. "What the fuck is that supposed to mean to me? Who are you?" My anger flares. I know Detra has kept me a secret, but for some reason it burns deep in my blood as I face this fact now. I'm here in front of someone who should know who I am. My nostrils flare, I hear my wife yell my name just as I reveal the truth.

"Cristó!"

"I am Detra's husband," I say smugly.

The gasps from my wife and her sister are audible. The little one standing before me— I'm not sure which sister she is— glares at me with her mouth hanging open. Detra rushes over to her sister's side.

"Jada, *por favor*, you have to keep this quiet for me. Just between *tu y yo*. No one will understand," my wife pleads.

I wrap an arm around her waist and tug her back into my chest. I feel her stiffen in my hold but I don't give a fuck. I've had enough of the games we've been playing. This just may work to my advantage.

"You're married? Have you lost your mind? Mommy and Papi are going to kill you," Jada says with wide eyes. "*Cuando?* How long have you been married?"

"It's been nineteen years going on twenty," I reply for Detra.

"Stop. Talking. Just…stop…talking," she says icily.

"Ah, hell nah, you've been married to this old man for how long?" Jada says before she pauses. "It all makes sense. You didn't get rich with Nelson. I'm the youngest. I watched it all. I knew it was bullshit."

"Jada!"

"No, no, you've lied to everyone. We're your family. Why? Yes, this dude has to be older than you but Papi has Mommy by nine years. I don't think it would have been a problem. He don't look that old."

"Coño, I'm dying my hair," I grumble.

Detra whips her head in my direction to glare at me. Pointing a finger at me, she says. "You will absolutely not. She's a baby. Everyone's old to her."

"Excuse me, I am not a baby," Jada huffs and pouts.

In this moment, she looks more like the younger version of Detra that arrived at my door making demands. However, that's not what brings a smile to my face and has my groin tightening. No, it's the fact that my wife has acknowledged her attraction to me whether she wants to acknowledge it or not.

"Enough, I have bigger things going on," Detra says sharply, killing my momentary satisfaction.

Nothing, and I mean, nothing should be bigger than us. Yet, she speaks of this Nelson as if he were more important than me, her husband. I don't like it.

Rage consumes me. I want to spank Detra's pretty round ass until she takes back the years of hiding me and putting me second when I should be first. It's irrational. I gave her this free rein, but it infuriates me now.

"Yeah, well, that's why I'm here. Nelson wants the access codes changed for the new systems I've been working on. He asked that I do it from the office on the secure computers," Jada says, still looking curiously between Detra and I.

"Yes, I knew he would." Detra sighs. "Wait, how did you get here so fast? I just hung up with Nelson."

I stiffen this time. Detra told me she wanted to step out of her office to go to the restroom. Not to go call another man.

Jada's checks start to glow. All of the tough girl from earlier melts away. She looks more like a little girl embarrassed in front of her big sister.

"I was around," she says shyly.

"Um, sure you were," Detra says suspiciously.

"So how long do I have to keep this a secret?" Jada says, a small grin taking over her lips as if she's just realizing she has the power here.

These Marques sisters are something else. My hand splays my wife's belly as I once again think of having our own niños. Jada's eyes fall to the gesture.

"It won't be much longer," I reply. "I would like to finally meet all of my in-laws."

"That's not going to happen," Detra bites out and steps out of my hold.

"*Sí*, it is. The question is, will it happen here or will they all be coming to Puerto Rico?"

"Wait, you've been hiding an entire husband. Old, but fine as fuck, husband in Puerto Rico all of this time?" Jada says and starts to laugh. "I can't wait to see Mommy react to this."

"Shut up. She's not going to react because there will be nothing to react to. This… it's not a real marriage. I mean, yes, I'm married to him, but it's not real," Detra says in exasperation.

"Sure looks real to me," Jada chuckles under her breath.

"It is very real. Your sister can deny me all she likes," I reach to brush my fingertips from my wife's temple, down beneath her chin and lift so her eyes are on me. "We are undeniable. She and I were meant to be."

I level Detra with a heated stare. I watch as her breath hitches and her breasts start to heave. The truth lies in her eyes. She knows my words are true.

"*Damn*," Jada drags out. "*Fuego.* The way he looks at you… *caliente.* That shit is so hot nobody in a ten-mile radius has dry panties. Oh, sis, that old man dick got you —"

"*Jada*," Detra seethes out in warning, turning to her sister.

"Okay, okay," Jada giggles. "I have work to get to. It was nice meeting you, Cristóbal. I can't wait to see you again."

After saying the last part, she rushes off before her sister can chide her again. Detra rounds on me with fire in her eyes. I can tell she's pissed.

"Stop telling people you're my husband," she hisses.

I crowd her space and lower until we are nose to nose. I can taste her anger on my tongue. Yet, it doesn't match my own.

"It is okay for killers across the country… all over the world to know you are my wife, but not your family? Why is this? Are you ashamed of me or you?"

She stumbles back as if my words have hit her physically. I take my own words in without the anger that clouds my mind and vision. I see something I've never seen before.

"You are ashamed," I say.

It spills out from my lips like bitter poison. I don't want to wait around for her reply. I feel a new level of betrayal as I turn and walk away.

"Cristó," I hear her call after me, but I don't stop.

Never once did I think she was ashamed of me, of us. It rips at something so deep, I feel like I can't breathe. And it hits me.

This is why I married my wife. So I'd never have my heart ripped out like this. Like my mother did my father.

CHAPTER TEN

Detra

I didn't know what to say. Cristóbal's question threw me. I never thought about how I feel about what I once felt I had to do.

Am I ashamed of my husband? No, I'm not ashamed of Cristó. He is a great man when you get to know him. He had a rough life that he keeps locked down deep.

He has shared things with me I know he has never told another. To say I'm ashamed of him would be so far from the truth. I admire him. I think he's the strongest man I know.

I am, however, ashamed of me. I have done things to protect those that I love that I'm not so proud of. If I had to air my dirty laundry, I'd bury my head in the sand.

I could never tell my father what his actions caused me to do. I did what I felt was right to save a really fucked up situation. Yet, forming that explanation into words is harder than I ever

75

thought it would be because I never thought about the shame I feel about the things I've done and would do all over again.

Without. Question.

"Cristó," I try as we pull up in front of Manny's home.

"We will go inside and talk to my brother. When we are done, I will be staying here with him. You do what you need to do to secure our investments.

"I will handle some things that have been weighing on my mind about all of this," he says, then steps out of the car without even a glance in my direction.

I swallow that lump in my throat and fight back tears. I don't cry. I never show my weakness. And here I am wanting to burst into tears over this man again.

I nod as if he's still sitting with me to see. Inhaling deeply, I shove it all back in. I will not fall apart. This is what I wanted.

So why does it hurt so much?

Once I compose myself, I step from the car and meet Cristó on the curb. His lips are tight and his focus remains anywhere but on me. He places a hand on the small of my back, but before I can melt into the touch, he removes the warm palm.

It seems like he places a world of distance between us. I've never felt so far away from him. Not even with oceans between us.

"Ah, my favorite Suarez in the world. How are you sister? You are gorgeous as ever?"

"Do you have answers for us?" Cristó cuts off Manny's warm greeting with a cold tone.

"*Mi hermano*, what has you so uptight?" Manny asks with a frown marring his handsome face.

"I would like to get to the bottom of this. I'll be able to return Detra to her dear friend and I can go home," Cristó says.

I feel like a knife has just been plunged into my chest. The hollow sound in his voice is nothing like the man that talked of starting a family. The man that had been wearing me down.

"Okay, come. I have a few things I want to show you about the car," Manny says, eyeing his brother closely.

"I have a few calls to make. This is Detra's *job*. I will not get in the way. Just forward what you have so I'm aware of what's going on in my family business," Cristó says, before turning and leaving us.

I don't know what I'm more hurt by, his cold shoulder or the fact that he won't look at me. I stare at his back as he disappears into the house. I have no control over the shuddered breath I take.

"Trouble in paradise?"

"He is so stubborn. I don't know how to give him what he is asking for. I don't know how to express my feelings," I whisper.

Manny tosses a hand over my shoulder and squeezes. I sag into one of the two friends I've ever had. Nelson and Manny… *or am I wrong about that too?*

"You have always been able to express your feelings with my brother. I think the problem is you don't know how to express *these* feelings to him," Manny says gently.

"I made a mistake," I say through trembling lips. "This was never supposed to be real. I was never suppose…." I cut the words off and drag in some air.

"Ah, this is where you both had it wrong. You both wanted something other than what either of you allowed yourselves to see. It took way too long for you both to admit it to yourselves."

"I was a kid when I met him. I didn't know shit. I knew I'd do anything to save my family. I knew I was smart enough to figure things out as I went. All I needed was a chance. He gave me one," I say.

"But have you ever asked yourself why?"

I open my mouth, but nothing comes out. No, I never did. I just keep moving forward until I fixed the world for everyone without anyone knowing. I've had a double life for so long I haven't questioned a thing about it.

"Come, let's find us a rat," Manny says when I give no reply. "Then, we can get to the one that curled up Cristó's butt."

I can't help but crack a smile. I follow my friend and try my best to shove my heart back in the box it tried to jump out of. I don't have time for the roller coaster that's my marriage.

I don't like what I'm looking at one bit. I've gone through everything Manny has placed in front of me. I told Talina that when someone wanted to hurt Nelson they'd start with her.

Those two have barely figured out that they are in love with each other and it has started. I'm glad I ignored Nelson and started to dig into Talina's ex. I'm learning a lot from the file on him alone.

"So he has changed his patterns since she's been gone?" I ask.

"About a week after, he has been looking like a ghost is chasing him. He takes trips across town to Talina's place at least twice a week," Manny grunts.

"Do we know who's following him?"

"No, the guys' orders were to stay on Malcolm. The car following him is never the same and the plates are always different," he replies.

"So he could be bringing shit to her door and he doesn't know it," I huff and rub the bridge of my nose.

"You got it," he says.

"I want to know who's in those cars. Tell your guys not to lose them again, I want to know who they belong to," I say through tight lips.

"Do you think this is connected to Nelson?"

"Not ruling out anything. You said his phone records have him suddenly calling Talina's sister, but they never talked much before the break up. From what Talina told me, her sister didn't care much for him," I reply.

"Gotcha." Manny nods. "And what are you thinking about the service call?"

I move my hand to my temple and close my eyes. "I have no fucking idea. Nelson shouldn't have even been using that car. He was going to loan it to me before I changed my plans to head to Puerto…" my words trail off and I open my eyes wide.

"You were supposed to be riding in that car," Cristóbal's voice roars at my back.

Startled I turn to find him breathing like a bull as his hard glare pins me. I don't know how to take his reaction after earlier. He's vibrating with rage.

Faster than I can register the action, he has his phone in hand and at his ear. His jaw ticks as he waits for whoever to pick up. His free hand clenches and unclenches at his side.

"I have changed my plans again," he says into the phone. "No," he barks. "I will not be returning home. I will be where I'm needed until this bullshit is resolved."

His nostrils flare and his eyes narrow as he listens to the voice on the other end. His face starts to turn bright red with anger. His hand shoots up to tug at his tie.

"You have questioned me for the last time," he says in a deadly calm and hangs up.

"We could be here forever making a list of people that want you out of the way," Manny sighs, with frustration and anger in his voice.

"Then, we will be here forever," Cristó snarls. "I want a list of everyone that would have known about her travel plans. I want to know who feels comfortable enough to aim for *my wife.*"

A shiver runs through me. Something in the way he says the words takes on a new meaning. I don't want to dig too deeply so I turn my attention to Manny and the grim look on his face.

Who wants me dead? Ha! Everyone.

~B~

Cristóbal

"I don't like this," I say as we enter Detra's New York condo.

"I'm tired. I don't want to get on a plane tonight. This is not my primary residence. Few know about it," she says, sighing and rubbing the back of my neck.

"I don't mean the place."

"Then what?"

"Tell me again. How do you think the ex-boyfriend is connected to you?" I ask for the millionth time.

I know she's getting aggravated with the question. I also know that sometimes we can miss the little things. Asking repeatedly will yield an answer eventually.

"I told you already. I'm not so sure he is connected now that I believe the target is me," she replies.

I flinch hearing her say this. I have put the only woman I have ever loved in danger. I put her in a role that has always threatened her life without a second thought. I feel like such a bastard.

If it were up to me, I'd wrap her in my arms and take her back to Puerto Rico with me. Then, I'd find this cabrón that has dared to threaten her life and skin him alive.

"Please stop looking at me like that," she says, walking closer to stand before me.

I want to touch her, I want to take her lips and devour her. Yet, I won't. The only reason I have not gotten on a plane and flown away from here is because her life has been threatened. Otherwise, I would have left my wife to the life she wants to keep so badly.

The life where she doesn't have to be ashamed of her husband.

"I have not looked at you any way."

"Yes, you have. You wouldn't look at me before, but now you are looking at me as if I'm fragile and I can't handle myself," she says.

"I would like to get some rest," I say looking around the apartment.

"*Marido*," she says, causing my cock to twitch. "Look at me."

I look down into her brown eyes. She's more beautiful in this moment than she has ever been to me. I cup her face, unable to restrain myself any longer.

"I think you misunderstand my reaction to your question," she whispers.

"How so, *cariño?*"

"I have never been ashamed of you. At twenty, my fast ass used to fantasize about luring you into my bed. For years, I've measured every man I've date against my forbidden husband.

"You… you have been everything to me. A friend, a mentor, a savior. I couldn't ruin that with my wanton_curiosity. I can blame it on the alcohol if I want, but the truth is… I wasn't that drunk when you kissed me.

"I wanted you to. God, did I want you to. And when you did, everything made sense and didn't all at the same time. I've never been ashamed to be yours.

"My shame comes from knowing I'll never be a lady like the women you date. I have blood stains up to my neck. I've done things I can never wash away. And you know what... I don't think I regret a single one.

"For that I am ashamed because I will never be the wife you deserve," she says lowering her lashes.

I lift her head and search her eyes. I can see the truth bleeding from them. I haven't been the only one in this for the last nineteen years. Even before I knew I was in love with my wife, I'd fallen in love with her.

"I would have married a statue if that's what I wanted. You are the fire to my flame, *mi amor*. I can't wake without thinking of you—"

"But I can't be what you want. I don't know how—"

It's my time to cut her off. I crush her lips with mine. Leading and guiding her the way I've been doing since she walked into my life. I don't know how to love either, but for her I'm willing to learn.

"I should have done a lot differently with you," I breathe against her lips. "I will spend the rest of my life correcting my mistakes, *mi amor*."

I seal my mouth over hers before she tries to protest or change my mind. I sip from her lush lips as if it's the last time I'll ever get a chance to. My hands roam her back and ass.

I need her naked so I can make love to her. I know she's not ready for me to say the words, but I'm ready to say them to her with my body. Stroke by stroke, I want to sing her body a song that will teach her the depth of my love for her.

"Cristó," she whimpers when I move my lips to her neck and begin a trail down her throat.

Buttons fly as I rip her shirt open, the fitted white blouse ruined the way she has ruined my sanity. I'm mad for this woman. I wouldn't be satisfied if she were anything like the women I've fucked in my past.

Detra is so much more to me. She mirrors me in so many ways. She gives me hopes and dreams I never knew I wanted. Even now, my blood sears my veins, calling out for her to become one with me and my desires.

"Wait," she pants.

I release her enough to look into her eyes. I can see the desire within them. My brows draw in confusion.

"What?"

Biting her lip she searches my eyes. I don't know if a cold shower will work if she tells me this isn't what she wants. I'm bursting with need as it is.

"We've been having a lot of unprotected sex. I don't have condoms here," she says sheepishly.

I growl and lift her into my arms. "Bedroom, where?"

"Cristó," she laughs.

I capture the sound with my lips. "Where, *cariño?*"

"At the top of the stairs, at the end of the hall," she says breathlessly.

The thought of her swollen with my child has me ready to come in my pants like a thirteen-year-old. It is no mistake on my part that I have not been using protection. I want my wife.

I already admit to being a bastard. If a child is the only way I can get her to stay with me… so be it. I will have something her Nelson doesn't.

Her fingertips brush at the crease between my brow. "What is it? What are you thinking about?"

"Nothing," I say, pecking her lips as I climb the stairs.

"You're lying," she says in a knowing tone.

"It's nothing we need to talk about now. I have other plans for our mouths."

"Is that so?" The hunger in her eyes causes me to push forward faster.

Entering the bedroom, I move to the bed to drop her down on it. I pull off my suit jacket and drop it to the floor. I rip my shirt open just as I did hers. I have no patience for buttons.

Detra gets on all fours and crawls to me at the edge of the bed. She helps with my belt, freeing me from my pants. Before I can step out of my shoes and kick my things aside, she's on me.

I drop my head back and shove a hand in my hair. The feel and sound of her sucking me is too good not to relish. Never afraid to take me on, she gives head like it's a challenge to be met. And meet it she does.

"*Joder, sí,* just like that," I groan. "Taste every inch."

I cup her face with my free hand and start to rock my hips. The choking sound she makes as she tries to take me whole rings in my ears. I clench my teeth.

Her hands pump me as she back off, licking the tip. I'm not going to last if she keeps this up. I reach into her hair and tug her head back.

I bend to kiss her, savoring her swollen lips. Kicking off my shoes, I climb onto the bed. Detra moves back to give me room. She reaches to unfasten her skirt, getting it open just before I rip it and her panties down her legs.

I flip her onto all fours in front of me. I dive in for her core from behind. My thumb circling her tight ring of flesh. Her hips start to circle as she rides my face. I still her hips and push my face in deeper.

"Oh, yes, yes!"

"Tell me what this greedy pussy wants," I say, pushing two fingers into her.

I reach for my cock and squeeze. I want to wring pleasure from her at least once before I enter her. I can feel how close she is.

"She wants you. Don't make me beg," she purrs.

"She can always have me," I say, returning my mouth to her center.

I use my fingers and mouth to tip her right over. I don't know who enjoys it more. Although, Detra gives a good case for her own enjoyment with the screams that fill the room.

I look down at her body as she collapses and convulses against the mattress. She's beautiful lying on her stomach.

Covering her body with mine, I push inside of her. I drag my hands from her shoulders to her hands. We link our fingers as I start to move into her. She wiggles, giving me the perfect angle I need. I plant a foot into the bed and start to drive into her.

"So good," I groan.

"Always so good."

"Is it?" I breathe in her ear.

She shudders and moans, nodding her head. I nip at her shoulder, pushing in and out of her tight body. I don't know what life was before having a taste of my wife.

"That's it, drip all over me," I say, sticking my tongue in her ear.

Our hands tighten, my toes dig deeper. I push hard against her ass. Her cries get louder and I pump harder. The bed starts to rock under the force.

"Cristó, *Tómalo todo*," she calls.

"Don't say things you don't mean," I pant.

"I mean it. Take it all," she repeats in English.

She has just opened a door. I will do just that. For the rest of the night, I consume and devour my wife.

I. Take. It. All.

CHAPTER ELEVEN

Strange Calls

Detra

I'm half asleep with my phone ringing over my head. It's the third time this morning. I was hoping I'd get to catch a little sleep before having to get on the plane back to London.

I groan and reach for the phone. Once again it's an unknown number. I answer and place the phone to my ear.

"Hello."

This time I'm greeted by breathing before the line cuts off. Now they have my attention. I sit up in bed staring down at my phone. I dial Manny.

"What's up?" Manny answers sounding as exhausted as I feel.

"I don't know if you'll get a hit, but an unknown number keeps calling and hanging up. Third time this morning," I say as he answers.

"I don't like this," Manny snarls.

"Just see what you can find out," I reply and hang up.

I place the phone down and release a heavy breath. I can feel his eyes on me without turning around. This is not how I want my *Jefe* to see me.

"I have it under control," I repeat the words I told him all last night in between and after our makeup sex.

"Do you?" He says, reaching to rub my bare back.

"Yes."

"I want you to let me handle this. Manny was right. Your hands should no longer be dirty. Things have changed. You are building our legitimate businesses—"

I whip around to face him. "I am what I need to be for our family. Don't mistake my softness in your bed for softness in our business. I have this under control."

His lips tighten. Those hazel-blue eyes zone in on me. I know he doesn't like my tone, but I'm pissed. I've worked too hard to have him doubt me over this.

He gives a curt nod. "I will allow you time to sort this out. If I feel it's getting out of control… if I see you in harm's way, it ends."

"Thank you, *Jefe*."

I take note of his flinch. He has done that several times since yesterday. Something shifts in his gaze and he lifts to grasp my face between his fingertips.

"*Marido*, I'm your husband, not your boss," he says sharply.

"I had the understanding all this time that you are both," I challenge.

"Then as your *Jefe*, I'm going to spank your ass," he bites out.

"Not if you want your *huevos*, you won't."

"You drive me insane," he rumbles, flipping me onto my back.

For the rest of the morning we shut out the world. He fucks me tenderly. Yes, I'm still not able to admit he's making love to me.

I'm not ready for that.

~B~

Cristóbal

"I want to meet your family," I say, as I play with the hair at her temples.

We are finally on our flight heading back to London. I have so many things running through my head. I don't want to step on Detra's toes as my *Teniente,* but as her husband it's another story.

Every instinct within me tells me to protect her. I want to flush out this coward and handle this problem for her, but I know what that will do to her. It is my own fault that I even have to think about this.

"I don't think you really want that. Just imagine, five women that are all under five four with big mouths. My father... sometimes I think we drove him into his problems," she says, losing the humor at the end of her statement.

"I think I'd enjoy it," I laugh to lighten her mood again.

"I promise you wouldn't."

"Your father means a lot to you, but I still get the feeling you haven't forgiven him," I say cautiously.

"You know... I tried. You've been telling me to for years and I did try. But... I found out he started to gamble for a bit not long after I got him out of trouble.

"Y... you just don't do things like that to people you love and that love you. Mommy thinks his shit has never stunk a day in his life. I... they make me so mad," she says.

"Because they have a love you don't understand?"

She lifts her head and pulls away from me. I'm sorry I opened my mouth when I see the set of her jaw. She's beyond pissed at me.

"That's not love," she says in disgust. "To lie and put your entire family in trouble. He could have gotten us all killed. If it weren't for Nelson..."

She trails off and shakes her head. Actually tears spill down her cheeks. I tense at the sight of them and... the friend.

"We had a shitty childhood. No money, a fucked up neighborhood, but the one thing I always had in my home was my family. Papi was everything to me. I trusted him with everything in me.

"Those men that came to collect. They were going to rape me. Nelson came out of nowhere and fought with me until they ran off bleeding back to their boss.

"I had no choice but to run away. I made Nelson promise to leave his house and that bitch mother of his to hide. I went straight to Manny. I had to think fast and act faster before those guys went back for the rest of my family," she says as tears streak down her face.

"This is why my brother asked me to make that piece of shit, Russo, hold off on collecting his debt. If I would have known, I would have killed him and his men," I snarl.

"I didn't want that. In Jersey, me and my sisters survived by making examples. That's what my father taught us and that's what we taught Nelson when they picked on him for being the only white boy in the neighborhood.

"You make an example of one. When I found out what Papi was doing, I needed to do more than pay off his debt. I needed to make an example so no one ever fucked with him or my family again.

"I knew... I knew in my gut he wouldn't stop. So I needed a way to make an example. And I had to find a way to return the favor to Nelson. I owed him for saving my life," she says with a haunted look in her eyes.

"So you used me to make another man wealthy?"

"No, I used you to keep two kids alive. Nelson saved me and you saved us both. When you placed that power in my hands, I made sure everyone knew who I was. Russo and his men had nothing close to what you gave me.

"My family is not a part of our world so I was able to hide a lot from them, but those that lurk in the shadows, preying on young girls and lost men... they saw the example I made," she says.

The dark look that flashes in her eyes reminds me why I was drawn to her then. Pieces she has always held from me fall into place. I understand the woman before me so much more.

"Well, let's start with me meeting this Nelson. It's been long enough, don't you think?"

"Yeah, maybe," she says with a small smile.

Suddenly, her brows wrinkle. I feel the shift in the air. Detra's smile falls and she sucks in a deep breath.

"Talina... I spent the night hanging out at her apartment before she left for London with Nelson," she says as her eyes bounce as if she's looking through her own thoughts.

"This would connect you to the ex?"

"Yes, it could. They had just broken up. She lived with him," she says and nods.

"I don't like this," I say tightly.

"Neither do I."

CHAPTER TWELVE

Mine to Love

Detra

"Hold on a second," I say to Cristó.

I laugh at the text message on my phone from Talina. It feels so foreign to crack a smile these days that's not forced. Usually when I do, it's because of the woman that stole my best friend's heart.

Talina: *Tell him to let me out. I want to walk again someday.*

Nelson informed me days ago that he and Talina aren't ready to come up for air. Which honestly has been fine with me. I don't want Nelson to be alarmed by what I've discovered in the last few weeks.

The less time I'm around them the better. Although, meeting Nelson has come up a few times, thankfully, Cristó has been too busy to try to follow me around everywhere.

The company that serviced the car before Nelson arrived in London doesn't exist. The appointment was made by someone claiming to be from our New York office, but we're still not sure who, or if this is a fact. The staff here in London followed protocol. There was no way for them to know it was all bogus.

"As for Malcolm, we have yet to locate him since a day ago," I say finishing the conversation we were having before the text came in. "There hasn't been a sign of the cars that have been tailing him either. Not since we left New York."

"As if they already know our moves. I still think you should tell your friend that his employee is in danger. You say she makes a lot of money for us. How do we know this didn't start with her?"

I release a breath and level my eyes on my husband. I didn't want to put Nelson's business out there, but I think it's time to fill in some blanks. Cristó is not the enemy.

Besides, Nelson has already told me that he's pretty serious about Talina.

"Talina is a sweet girl. There is only one reason anyone would come after her," I say.

He lifts a brow. "What is this reason?"

"Nelson. They started a relationship after arriving here. People will use her to hurt him if they can, but she's not the cause of this."

"And we are sure her ex is not involved?"

"Can't say that yet. Although, he would be a pawn, not a major player. I don't even think he knows about their relationship," I muse.

"This is just some office fling?"

"No. This is not a fling. He wants to make her his wife," I say with a smile.

"Then you tell him," he says firmly. "He would want to know. I would want to know."

I go to tease him, but his phone rings. I watch my husband wondering how did so much change so fast. He has been so attentive since we arrived back in London.

"No, I'll do it myself," he snaps into the phone and hangs up.

"Everything okay?"

"Everything is fine. I just need to make a few changes," he says, nostrils flaring. "I wanted to surprise you with a gift. My assistant is having trouble collecting it. Come, you and I will go collect it and get some fresh air."

"Actually, you can still surprise me. I'll stay here and you go. I'm waiting for a call and I'd love a bubble bath to relax some of this tension," I say, rolling my neck.

He looks at me, a war happening in those intense eyes. Standing, he pulls me from my seat. I look up at him, expecting him to protest.

"When I return I'll help you relax," he croons in a sexy promising tone.

He kisses my forehead gently, instead of taking my lips the way I expect him to. When I think about it, I guess that's a good idea. He'll never leave if we so much as brush lips.

"I look forward to it, old man," I purr.

I yelp when he slaps my ass. I laugh as he scowls at me. With one last squeeze of the cheek he just caused to sting, he turns and leaves from the brownstone he rented for us.

Unfortunately, the call I'd been waiting for comes as soon as Cristó leaves. I spend the next hour rolling my eyes at the voice on the other end of my phone. When I finally hang up, I go to have that bath I've been wanting.

The doorbell rings and I groan. All I want is that bath. I move towards the door, but it dawns on me that there shouldn't be anyone ringing this bell.

My husband made that clear. Not even his assistant has come by. Alonso has been Cristó's shadow for a few years now. It says a lot that not even he has had access to me.

I reach under the little table by the door were I strapped a gun and silencer beneath. Something tells me this is not a time to rely on my blades. The hairs are standing up on the back of my neck and arms.

Making quick work of the silencer, I slide to the door as the bell rings again. I move the curtain back slightly to see someone in a delivery uniform with a large bouquet of flowers in his arms.

"Someone fucked," I snort under my breath.

I'm allergic to roses. Cristó knows this. He had his rose gardens pulled and banned the gardener from planting them years ago. I thought it was overkill then. Sweet, but overkill as I was never there much, but he insisted.

Since my husband is the only one to know I'm here, I know for damn sure he didn't send me roses. Nelson would know better as well, but even he doesn't have this address as per my husband's wishes.

I shift, unlocking the door, ready to put a bullet in this guy's head. As soon as the lock disengages the door is pushed in on me. I stumble, but hold my aim.

"You picked the wrong day to deliver," Cristó hisses in the guy's ear as he shoves him into the house.

My eyes grow wide. Cristó kicks the door closed behind him and shoves the gun he took from the guy before him into his waistband. Lifting his own gun from the guy's back, Cristó places it to his temple. If he didn't look so sexy coming to my rescue, I might be mad he stole my thunder.

"Who sent you?" Cristó and I say in unison.

My husband looks at me with wild eyes. I see the small hint of a smile on his lips. I get the feeling he's enjoying the moment.

"Should I let you handle this?" I ask, returning the smile.

"It has been awhile since we have done this together. We'll take him down to the cellar," he says, shoving the guy forward.

~B~

Cristóbal

"I want you to return to Puerto Rico," I say as I walk up behind my wife.

I look at our reflections in the mirror. Her naked while rubbing cream into her skin. Me with a towel around my waist.

I place my hands on her hips and plant a kiss on her shoulder. Her silence is worse than her rejection. I know what this means.

"You will be protected in my home," I say when she still says nothing. "Detra."

"I will not run and hide. That is not who I am. He couldn't even give us a name, so why the hell should I run? I don't know who I'm running from. Who says your home is safe?"

"Enough, this is not a request," I says as my patience snaps in two.

She spins to face me, looking up through narrowed eyes. I don't care if she's angry. Returning to find someone outside our front door. A gun hidden in that bouquet of roses.

It took everything in me not to blow his head off first and ask questions later. My blood boils even now. The thought of losing Detra makes me crazy.

"Have I not held things down since I was nineteen? Hell, at eighteen I was running shit. You want me to run now?" Her voice breaks. "You think I've become soft, that I am weak?"

"No," I say tightly.

"Then, what has changed? Why do you treat me now as if I'm breakable?"

"Detra," I warn.

"No, tell me," she demands.

"Because I'm in love with you. *Te amo.* I love you so fucking much I feel crazy. I'm not here to just fuck you and have a good time.

"I followed after you because I'm tired of not having my wife by my side. But now I see the world I've sent you out into. I've taken off the fairytale glasses. I see.

"I have placed my princess in the center of the monsters while I've been up in the ivory tower," I say bitterly. "I'm not worthy of you, but I can't live without you any longer. If that means I have to spend the rest of my life slaying fucking dragons, so be it."

"You can't love me," she says with her head down.

"Coño, you have to be fucking kidding me," I bellow.

Taking her face in my hand, I tilt her head back and seize her lips. I kiss her with the passion of a man willing to die for the love of the woman that owns his heart.

Her hands go into my hair. I back her into the corner top and left her onto it. I tear my towel away and step between her thick thighs. Forcing myself to pull my lips away from hers, I start to kiss down her body.

I worship every inch of her skin. Showing with my mouth the love and devotion I have for her. I look up through my lashes to make sure she can see the love I have for her.

"*Te amo*. I love everything about you," I croon against her skin.

"How?"

"How can I not? I love this scar," I lick the flesh on the outside of her thigh. "Do you remember how you got it? I was furious with you for fighting with my men. They should've known better than to let you join in.

"You wouldn't shed a tear. You held your head high and let me stitch it for you. I think I fell more in love with you that day," I say against the mark.

I kiss my way to the apex of her thighs. Placing a kiss on her mound, nuzzling the flesh. I grin and lift my gaze to hers again.

"You were such a little thing when you came to me. All ass, no tits. Still not yet a woman," I chuckle. "The year after we married you returned and you were all woman, all curves. I started to crave you then.

"I wanted to taste you to see if you tasted as good as you looked. You didn't know you were driving me crazy even then," I say, pushing her legs further apart and dipping in for a taste.

I groan as her flavor bursts on my tongue. She tastes better than I ever imagined in those days. I scoop her ass into my hands and lift her up and closer to me.

"Cristó," she cries out.

I look at her to find her hands press to the mirror behind her, her body bowed in the air as I feast on her. I lift her higher and consume her more. My fingernails bite into her skin.

I keep eating until I feel her juices wash down my throat. Only then do I release her to sit back on the countertop. I take her lips, allowing her taste herself.

I kiss her so deeply my tongue is at the back of her throat. I've never wanted someone more. I want to be a part of her, inside of her. I want to absorb her into me and keep her safe within my own skin.

"I need you," I breathe.

"Please."

Tugging her body to the edge, I push into her waiting heat. I start to move inside of her, but this isn't enough. I need to be closer, deeper.

I pull out and look down at her pussy in awe. My brows draw. I don't know if it's so good because I'm madly in love with her or if she just has the best pussy in the world. I think it's a bit of both.

"Come," I say, lifting her from the counter.

I carry her into the bedroom, but I don't make it to the bed. I press her back to the wall and take her mouth. She clings to my shoulders giving as good as I'm giving.

I break the kiss to look into her eyes. She pushes at my chest and I let her legs fall to the floor. Turning her back to me, she bends at the waist and places her hands out for mine.

I line my cock up with her entrance and push in. Reaching for her hands, I lace my fingers with hers. I start to push in nice and slow.

I bite my lip and narrow my eyes as she starts to roll her hips against me. My eyes roll into the back of my head. I move our joined hands to her hips and take control of the push and pull.

"You like that? Do you feel my love for you?"

Detra

Oh, I feel him. I feel him in every cell of my body. I shudder as his voice rolls over me. I want to answer him, but my words are caught. I can only make a sound that comes out somewhere between a moan and a choking sob.

I feel like fire is burning through my veins. With each stroke he threatens to fan the flames to consume me whole. It's a death that I'm willing to accept at the moment.

"How can I not love you?" he asks against my skin before licking up my back.

He releases one of my hands to reach into my hair and tug my head back. He starts to pick up the pace and I swear the room starts to spin.

There are men that have sex and can scratch an itch and there are men that hit it right every single time. I mean that slow burn, hard hitting, fast fucking, bring it all together to end your life kind of sex. That's my husband.

My teeth chatter, my juices have my thighs drenched, and I feel the tingle of my orgasm everywhere. My scalp hums, my skin buzzes. I'm so close.

I've never felt like this with anyone else. I look over my shoulder to find him watching my ass. I grin and flex my cheeks, then clap my ass around him.

"Fuck," he roars and slaps my ass.

Releasing my other hand, he plants his palm to the wall. He reaches for one of my legs and tucks it into his side. I cover his hand that lands on my hip with my hand. His fingers flex, nails digging in.

"Ah, I'm coming, Papi. Keep fucking me just like that," I cry out.

"Yes, that's it. Come for me. Give it all to me," he groans. "Fuck that cock. Give me my pussy."

I come from his dirty words alone. I sag forward. Cristó leans into me.

"I want you in my bed. You will not walk in the morning and you will know my love from the inside out," he whispers.

I shiver and my heart leaps. I know I must be crazy. My body already feels the signs of his type of love, but I'm eager for more.

"Promises, promises, old man."

"This again," he chuckles. "We will see who is old. You will need sleep before me."

CHAPTER THIRTEEN

Abroad Again

Detra

Cristó insisted we meet with Nelson. Since I've been holding back from telling Nelson what's truly been going on, Cristó decided he will. I don't know how I feel about this, but then again, I don't know how I feel about anything.

I don't know why I'm so nervous. You'd think I were taking my first boyfriend to meet my family. I never realized how much I wanted these two to know each other.

"I have never seen you like this," Cristóbal says, placing a hand on the small of my back as we wait for someone to open the front door.

I have a key but for some reason I decided to ring the bell. Ms. Cork opens the door with a warm smile and I relax a little, ignoring Cristó's comment altogether. I can feel his eyes on me, but I keep moving.

"Mr. Fisher and Ms. Valentine will be down in just a moment," she says. "Can I take your things? Would you like some tea?"

"I think we're fine for now," I say as Cristó takes my coat from my shoulders to offer her.

"Hey, you," Talina sings as she appears.

"Hey," I reply pulling her into an embrace.

I have a death grip on her as we hug. She's going to be my lifeline tonight. When we pull apart, she gives me a curious glance. I shrug and flip my hair over my shoulder, trying to play it cool.

Get it together, Detra.

"There you are," Nelson booms as he jogs down the stairs.

Cristó wraps an arm around my waist, pulling me into his side. I have always understood that a part of Cristó is jealous of Nelson. He has nothing to worry about.

I've never seen Nelson that way. He has always been like family. When he came to help me that day it only solidified that brother-sister bond.

"Nelson, Talina, this is my husband, Cristóbal," I say starting the introductions. Nelson's brow shoots into his hairline. "Cristó, this is my best friend, Nelson and his girlfriend, Talina."

"It is a pleasure to meet you both," Cristó says.

"Yes... it is nice to meet you," Nelson replies shaking off his shock.

Nelson has been on a need to know basis for all of these years. He knows Manny, but not what Manny truly does. If I ever went down for my connections to Cristóbal, I didn't want Nelson to know enough to drag him down too. It's the way things needed to be.

I look at the two men. They are so completely different from each other. Yet, the same in more ways than I've ever noticed. Nelson holds Talina protectively at his side just as Cristó has me.

Cristóbal was right. I need to be the one to tell Nelson what's going on. He would want to know that I'm on alert for a viable threat concerning Talina. I owe my friend that.

"Cristó, Talina, do you mind if I steal Nelson away for a minute. I need to have a talk with him," I say.

"No problem. I get to pick your husband's brain," Talina says with a smile.

"Not sure there is much to pick, but I'm always willing to give my attention to a beautiful woman," Cristó says smoothly.

I stifle my laugh when Nelson stiffens and tugs Talina closer. I don't even think he knows he has done it. In response, Cristó palms the back of my neck, turning me to him.

My toes curl in my shoes as he makes it clear that I'm the only one he's here for. I'm quite sure he's also staking a claim as he leaves me breathless.

"Wow, you two are beautiful together," Talina says in awe.

"The old man is not so bad," I tease as I catch my breath.

Cristó slaps my ass and grunts down at me. He leans into my ear and says for my ears only. "*Te mostraré el viejo, esposita.*"

"I'm counting on it, *Marido*," I reply, rolling my gaze over his body.

I almost don't want to walk away as his eyes ignite. Damn, this man has me all types of strung out on him. I never thought anyone would have me like this.

He leans into my ear again to heatedly say. "*Te amo, mi amor.*"

I bite my lip and turn to walk away before I say or do something to embarrass us both. Yes, I love my husband. I'm just not ready to tell him.

~B~

Cristóbal

"I knew there was something different about her when she returned," Nelson says, pulling me from my musing.

I've been standing by the bar observing and drinking Brandy. Removing yourself from the picture can give you a broader view. I've been waiting for the day I'd get to see this Nelson and my *Esposita* interact.

"What do you mean?" I ask, not able to tear my eyes away from my wife.

"When she returned with all that money and… there was something in her eyes. I knew there was more behind it all. I just never pushed.

"Then the… emptiness. I was confused by it because she dated all those guys. She never cared about them.

"It was like they irritated or frustrated her more than anything. She just didn't see it. I don't know. It was like she was looking for something," he muses.

"That would be my Detra. Always looking for what's right in front of her. We are alike in that respect," I chuckle.

"But last year, when she turned up on my doorstep drunk. Something was different. Whoever the guy was this time. He actually made it through to the real Detra. He had cracked into her heart.

"Now I get it. It was you. Something changed between you two," he says as if he's solved a great puzzle.

"Does this anger you?" This time I do pull my eyes away to look this man in his.

"Not like you seem to be implying. She's all the family I have. I wouldn't have shit if it weren't for her. But now I have to wonder what she did to give me my shot at life," he says tightly.

I tilt my head. All evening I've watched my wife show this man in front of me unrestrained affection. Is it passionate affection? No, but it's still an open love I've never seen her give to anyone else, not even her sister in our brief passing.

I long for what I see between the two. Yet, I can see that they regard each other with the fondness of siblings. He is here to protect her.

"I don't explain myself to anyone. But because she has told me that you once saved her life. I will make this exception.

"I have always cared for Detra. I just didn't realize I'd fallen in love with her. Last year… I acted on my feelings. I always knew we would make fire, but I didn't know she'd consume me.

"I love my wife. She won't allow herself to admit it, but she loves me too. I'll do anything for her. Which includes giving her access to the world.

"I gave her that before she gave her body to me. You can rest your conscience, your business is built off of many sins, but sex is not one," I say and take a sip of my drink.

"You are right. She does love you. A year ago, I don't think she knew that herself. But she's getting there," he says with a grin.

"You look like you are in love," I say, nodding towards a laughing Talina.

"Yes, like you I've waited a long time for her to see me," he says in a haunted tone.

"*Sí*, they will kill you with the wait, but it is worth it in the end, no?"

"Yes, it is," he says with a face splitting smile.

I know that look. I release a laugh and slap him on the back. I still harbor a little jealousy towards this man, but he has shown he wants what's best for my *Esposita*.

"To the women we love and that drive us crazy," I say lifting my glass.

"Ha! To the women we love and Detra," he laughs.

"Salute," I chuckle. "It is agreed then that she drives us both crazy."

"Yes, I'm hoping to see more of you. I don't think it's fair I have to carry the load on that one."

"*Sí*, you will be seeing more of me. Although, she has a way of making me crazy from a long distance. Trust, *amigo*. You are not in this alone," I reply.

"She's looking at us. I think we should separate so she doesn't come for our balls," he whispers.

I laugh as my wife glares and her friend hurries away from me. He moves to Detra's side and whispers something in her ear. For the first time, I don't tense when he gets near her.

Detra nods and turns to me with a soft look on her face. Nelson turns back towards me and raises his glass. I nod at him.

Seeing them together, I wonder if getting Detra to stay with me will be so easy after all. Theirs is a bond that will be unbreakable. A few weeks ago that had been my intention. To break up this friendship that calls her away from me.

The information I wanted was to help me do so. Now, I've seen what Detra calls her freedom. I've seen the woman she's become outside of the gilded cage I've scheduled to place her in. I've come to find that I love her more with her wings spread.

"What's wrong?" Detra asks as she walks over and places her hands on my chest.

"Nothing at all."

"That's not what your face says."

"I am old. My thoughts take me away to far places in my old age," I tease, pulling her body flush with mine.

"I'm sorry," she says more seriously.

I knit my brows, searching her eyes. I'm confused by the apology and concern in her gaze. I begin to rub soothing circles against her back.

"What are you sorry for?"

"I've excluded you from our group. You've been over here by the bar lost in your own world," she replies.

"You have not excluded me from anything, *mi amor*. I have just been observing and taking things in."

"What are you taking in?"

"Your freedom," I reply.

"What if I told you it's not as appealing anymore?"

I cup her face between my hands and kiss her tenderly on the lips. Her lashes flutter and her cheeks begin to glow. I kiss her nose, allowing my lips to linger.

"I'd say we should sit down and talk. No more chasing and no more running. We'll talk the way we used to. How does that sound?"

"I can talk," she says with a little grin.

"*Perfecto.*"

CHAPTER FOURTEEN

Called Away

Detra

"Valentine's day is coming. What would you like to do?" Cristó asks as he draws the soapy sponge across my breasts.

"Greece sounds perfect."

"Greece it is," he replies.

"I have work to do. I can't run off to Greece."

He scoffs and drops the sponge, running his hand up the center of my chest. I shiver even though I'm not cold. I tilt my head as he plants a kiss behind my ear.

"Work has never held you in place. Finish what you need. We are going to Greece for Valentine's."

"Um, I'll think about it."

"*Esposita*, be my Valentine and come with me to Greece," he croons in my ear.

"Now when you put it that way."

"All of my grey hair is because of you," he groans.

"Lies."

He chuckles and wraps his arms around me. I could get used to this. We fall back into a comfortable silence, only broken by the sound coming from the other room.

"Your phone is ringing again," I say lazily.

Cristó grunts into my hair but doesn't move. I stay settled against the warmth of his chest. The water in the bathtub is nice and warm as well.

It's been so long since I've been so relaxed. I know it has a lot to do with the fact that I've accepted that I love Cristó. It took Nelson whispering— it's time for me to let go, but most of all, it's safe to do so— for me to fully admit it.

"It could be important," I say as I listen to the sound in the distance.

"My world is right here in my arms," he says and gives a gentle squeeze. "Leave that world out there for now."

"You truly think you are king. We have to answer you immediately, but you keep us all at bay when you please," I say with a smile.

"*Sí*, you finally get it," he says with mirth in his voice.

"What am I going to do with you?" I giggle.

"You are going to have this talk with me," he replies, moving his hands to my shoulders.

I sigh. I knew that was coming. I walked right into.

"What do we do?"

"I will tell you what I want. I want you by my side. We don't have to decide where that is for now. I just don't want to wait for you to appear twice a year," he says.

"I can move it to three times a year," I tease.

He makes a growling sound and nips my ear. I shrink away trying to block him, water splashes around us and my heart swells. The words are on the tip of my tongue, but I can't say them.

"I will allow you to leave me to go wherever you want three times a year," he says.

"Is that right?" I look up over my shoulder at him. "You will allow me to leave?"

"*Sí*," he nods. "You have heard me. We will be together from now on. When you want this freedom you crave, I will allow you to go."

"Um, I think you have made a mistake. I will be with my husband out of choice. If I want to travel, whenever I want to travel, it will be out of choice," I retort.

"We will agree to disagree for now."

"Some talk," I snort.

"Stand up and bend over. I'm sure that conversation will go better," he croons in my ear.

I lift a brow at him. He gives me a pointed look letting me know it's a command, not a request. I stand and bend just as he says, water cascading from my body.

As soon as I do, the sound of the doorbell fills the house. I lift and I'm already in route to my gun. Cristóbal is out of the tub and past me before I can make good tracks.

"Stay here," he says low, tossing me a towel to cover with.

His phone rings again, this time he answers it. I relax once he starts barking at Alonso on the other end.

"Alonso, if I do not answer that means I'm busy. That does not mean for you to show up here to disturb me," he snarls.

"No, I'm not coming down to let you in. What is it?"

I shake my head and go to shower off. I'll let him deal with his assistant.

~B~

Cristóbal

I throw things into a bag in frustration. I have business to attend to back home. I don't understand how I suddenly have so many incompetent people around me.

"Can I help with anything?" Detra asks as she sits beside my bag, watching me.

"I would tell you to kill them all but that's not your department," I seethe.

"Say the word," she says with a grin.

I pause and look at me wife. The wickedness I see in her eyes tugs at something in me. I toss the shirt in my hand aside and move to stand between her legs.

I bend and capture her lips. Craving her taste, I miss her already. I'm not ready to leave her.

"Tell me again why I agreed to leave you behind," I say against her lips.

"I have business here. I want to spend Valentine's Day in Greece with you, like you promised. That means wrapping up here. You promised to return as soon as you straighten things out. A day or two tops," she purrs against my lips.

"I don't like it. It's a day or two too long. Pack your things," I demand.

"I don't like it either, but I have to be in this meeting with Nelson and Talina in the morning. You said this can't wait that long," she says with that gorgeous pout on her lips.

"You are right." I sigh. "Come see me out. Lock up as soon as I'm gone."

We move to the lower level, where we say our goodbye and I take one last taste of her mouth. It's a lingering one. I don't feel this is right, but I push the feeling aside.

She has agreed that we will be together. The chase and wait are over. Pressing my lips to her forehead, I release her.

"*Te amo, Esposita.* I will return as soon as possible."

"I know you will," she says. "See you soon, *Marido.*"

I climb in the back of my car headed to my jet. Thoughts of Detra fill my head. She has become so much more to me.

I can't remember ever feeling this detached from life before. Just the thought of being away from her again causes an ache in my chest. I rub at it, but it doesn't go away.

Something just feels off. I take out my phone to call her just to check in, but I pause. My thoughts turn in a different direction as I see all of the missed calls on my phone.

"*Atención,*" I mutter to myself.

I need to focus. Things aren't adding up. For one, Alonso wouldn't be the one to call for such matters. His excuse for doing so doesn't make sense. His calls are the only missed calls I have on my phone.

I close my eyes to still the rage that rises in me. Details I've been subconsciously cataloging come back to me. My pursuit of my wife had me placing one too many facts on the back burner.

I settle back into my seat. As cool as a man can be. At least on the outside.

I make a call and place the phone to my ear. I don't so much as narrow my eyes as Alonso stiffens in the front passenger seat. I'm hyperaware of everyone's movements.

"*Jefe,*" the voice on the other end answers.

"¿*Cómo está mi pequeño asesino favorito?*"

"I am well, but I know not of this little killer you speak of. I am a simple bookstore keeper, traveling to find more rare books," she says in her raspy voice.

I smile. I don't blame my brother for falling for her and keeping it from me. Love will make you do things you never thought you would.

"Am I right?"

"*Sí*, you are very right."

"Who?"

"I don't know yet who helps him, but I will know soon. Would you like me to take care of it?"

"I believe I will get the opportunity to do this one myself," I reply, my focus on the head in front of me as its owner strains to hear my conversation.

"You have told my wife about this?"

"*No, Jefe.* I see you're still angry with me for that call. Forgive me."

"It is forgiven," I reply.

"You underestimate her, *Jefe*, but I've learned that is a thing with you Suarez men."

"*Sí*, I may. Finish up, it's time for you to take a vacation. Your *niño* misses you."

She chuckles and hangs up without a word. I end the call and reach into my bag, placing one hand around cold steel and the other around a marble hilt.

"It will be good to go home," I say calmly. "Maybe I have been neglecting a few things."

"Soon, things will be as they should," Alonso says.

My muscles bunch, but I show no expression on my face. His tone alone has me itching to slice his throat, but I'm a man of more patience than people know. I will let this take it's course.

"*Sí*, that I can guarantee," I say darkly.

I'm always ready. Are you?

~B~

Detra

I start to daydream about Greece as I rub lotion into my skin. I'm going to miss Cristó, but I'm looking forward to the trip he promised.

This will just be a day or two. I can handle that. I look down at my phone with a smile expecting a text from my husband. My smile falls when I see it's Gabriella.

> **Gabriella:** *Alonso can't be trusted. Just got off call, something is not right with Jefe.*
> **Me:** *Where are you?*
> **Gabriella:** *In a SUV outside your front door.*
> **Me:** *Coming.*

I leap from the bed without another thought. I'm dialing and trading my pajama shorts and tank for jeans and a T-shirt. I'm annoyed that it takes more than two rings for my call to be answered.

"What's up, cuz? What do you need?" Emilio croons into the phone.

"I'm linking my phone to you. Find me and bring everything and everyone you've got," I say and hang up.

I said I keep my family in the dark about certain things. I never said that they're not with the shits. Today, we're all going to get our hands dirty. No one, and I mean no one, fucks with Cristobal Suarez without answering to me.

"*Cabrón* got me all the way fucked up," I mumble to myself as I check my clips and head for the door. "This is why you let me run shit, *Jefe*."

~B~

Cristóbal

I can feel the shift as we pull into the airplane hangar. So this is the day they want me to die? Too bad I have not agreed with this plan.

"Take me back," I command.

I know that I'm safe in this armored car. I will put a bullet in these two before they change that fact. I step out of this vehicle and I'm vulnerable and without back up.

Alonso may have had a wise plan if he were dealing with someone else. The driver starts to obey my command. However, Alonso starts to sputter in his seat.

"Don't, we have a flight. *Jefe*, we need to get on the plane—argh!" Alonso screams as I slam the blade of my knife into his shoulder.

"Shut your fucking mouth," I seethe. "You think I'm stupid? I will show you stupid.

"I never told you where I was staying. How did you show up at my door? Why have you been trying to place doubt in my head about my *Teniente*?

"Do you think I haven't noticed? '*Jefe, maybe she is losing her control?*' '*Are you sure you can trust her with this?*' All of this has been reasons for me to doubt her. That is how you orchestrated it to look, *sí*?"

"Please," he cries out as I lean into the blade.

"Shut up," I snarl. "You were the one I asked for those reports about Nelson Fisher and Fisher, Inc. Nelson and Detra's troubles started after this request.

"You would have been able to find out about the car. It was your job to find out Detra's plans and tell me, but you never did, did you? You kept the information for yourself.

"What happened, Alonso? She surprised you as much as me showing up on my doorstep for Christmas?"

"She rules you."

"Why is that your business?" I seethe. "You are always sticking your nose in things that don't concern you. Now today, this panic you bring.

"Why would Manuel or Stony contact you? I have no missed calls. Your mistake this entire time was thinking that pussy had me so distracted I don't see *you*. *¿Quién es estúpido ahora?*"

"You don't deserve any of this," he cries out. "You give that *Puta* more control than your own family. I get rid of you then I can get rid of her and your weak brother."

"Again, you show how foolish you are," I hiss and twist the blade in his shoulder. "Everyone has their place. I haven't had the *policía* in my business in years and none of my loyal men or women have had problems.

"You are entitled. It is my fault. I shouldn't have hired the brother of some *Puta* I was just fucking," I snarl.

"Loyalty," he pants. "You don't know loyalty. She was in love with you, but you never saw that. My sister deserved better."

"And I gave her better. I introduced her to her husband. She is happy. Why is this my problem?"

"He is poor," he retorts.

"You are a fool. Your sister is not poor or wanting. You are just greedy," I say to him. Turning my attention to the driver I bark. "I told you to drive!"

Things go to shit in the blink of an eye. Alonso aims and fires at the driver and I put a bullet through Alonso. I'm trapped in the back of this car with two options. Sit and wait out my car being ambushed or open the door and take my chances.

My body is too big to climb into the front seat in this vehicle. Before I can make a decision, they begin to open fire. When I find out who is behind this—who gave Alonso the confidence to try this—I'm going to kill them slow, very slow.

The bulletproof car holds its weight, but that's not going to last for long. My anger is at a boiling point. Suddenly, I hear the screech of tires and a shift in the gunfire.

My phone rings and my gut tells me to answer.

"We're here, *Jefe*. Stay down," Detra's voice comes through the line.

"Get out of here," I demand.

"I don't think so. This is my chance to return the favor. I'm saving your life."

"I am telling my wife to get the fuck out of here," I bellow.

"And I'm telling my husband, I'm not leaving without him. Now let me focus. People are shooting at us," she says and cuts the call.

"*Detra*," I roar.

I grab my gun and reach in my boot for the other one resting there. Releasing the door, I kick it open and start to fire. I will not leave my wife uncovered.

~*B*~

Detra

That man has bumped his head if he thinks I'm leaving without him. I come out of the car blasting. Emilio and the others have already begun to clear a path to the Rolls incasing my husband. I'm not even going to stop to think about the big shit Gabriella pulls out as she starts to blast.

I bite back a string of curses when I see Cristó emerge from the car like a mad man. His focus is on taking down anyone aiming at me.

"Get down," I bark at him.

He gives me a death glare and rushes toward me, firing over me. I continue to fire as the others cover us both. We need to get out of here before local authorities arrive.

Cristó plucks me up like a doll, placing me on his waist. I grind my teeth in annoyance, but I take advantage of my new height. I fire to protect us as he continues for the SUV I just hopped out of.

"Let's go," he bellows to my crew.

Gabriella jumps in the driver's seat. I tighten my lips when Emilio jumps in with blood dripping from his shoulder. I want to get out and shoot at more of them.

"It looks like a graze. I will call in a favor. I know someone," Cristó says against my temple before kissing it, after leaning in to look Emilio over. "Never do that again."

"I will do all your personal hiring from now on and I'll find out who was responsible for this," I say coolly. "Then, I'll never have to do this again."

"Coño, it's time to talk about retirement. You, Gabriella, and I will be having a chat," he says sternly.

"Whatever you say, *Jefe*."

"*Marido*."

"Yeah, that too."

"I hear you talking about me, Jefe," Gabriella calls over her shoulder.

"Stubborn women. My brother should listen to me."

Gabriella makes a sound in the back of her throat. I wonder what that's about, but I keep my focus on my husband. He is safe. That's what matters.

CHAPTER FIFTEEN

Bad Company

Detra

"So all of this was about you and Cristóbal?" Nelson says as I sit in his London office.

My husband and I are off to New York to check on something before we can head out for our vacation in Greece in two weeks. All the pieces fit together, but one. Neither I nor Cristó feel we have sealed the lid on this one.

"As far as we know so far. I'll have more details soon. Forget all of that. When are you going to propose?"

"In two weeks, on Valentine's day," he says with a grin.

I give a low whistle. "That's big," I say, returning his smile.

This is huge for him. Valentine's day has always been a horrible day for him. A reminder of that bitch mother of his.

"Yes, it is."

"I'm happy for you. If anyone deserves this it's you," I say.

"Yet, you still don't believe in love?"

"I never said I don't believe in it. I just never wanted to deal with the pain of it," I murmur.

"Here's the thing. You really have no control over it."

"Okay, time for me to go. Just because you're in love doesn't mean everyone else has to be," I say and get up to collect my things. "Tell Talina I'll see her soon."

"You can't run from the truth," he calls after me.

"Sure you can, I've been doing it all of my life," I say over my shoulder.

"I still love you."

I stop and turn. I try to keep the emotions out of my voice. "My brother, my friend. You have more love from me than I know how to give. There's only one man that rivals that."

"So you admit you love him," he taunts.

"I'll see you soon, Nelson."

I turn and leave with a smile on my face.

~B~

Cristóbal

"Still no word on the ex-boyfriend?"

"No, *hermano*."

"Talina means a lot to my wife. I've watched them together. If this will hurt Talina, it will hurt my wife. I don't like having this loose end," I grumble. "Find him."

"So we're not going to talk about what happened?"

"No, it is done. Gabriella has named the one I need to see," I reply.

"And if they have the ex?"

"Either way they are finished."

"But you don't believe they do. Something still doesn't fit for you. I can hear it in your voice," he says.

"Nothing is ever as it seems. We will have answers. We'll allow this dust to settle, then we can get to the rats that are still hiding."

"Everything has changed, hasn't it?"

"*Sí*, I have taken my head out of the sand. I don't know if I can allow this to continue this way," I speak the thoughts that have been haunting me.

"I hear you. You both will do what's right. Anything you need. You tell me," he says.

"I will see you soon. We will discuss what I need from you then."

"*Adiós, hermano*," he says on a sigh.

"*Adiós.*"

Be Mine

Detra

Easter...

"Why are you in here alone looking so sad?" Papi asks as he walks into the den.

I've been angry with my parents for a long time, but I've always made sure they're okay. This house was the least I could do to repay them for the good times.

"Everyone says I'm cranky and Cristó has been with you all damn day," I huff and pout.

"*Sí*, they are right. You are grumpy," my father chuckles. "I think I'm more excited about your *niño* than I was for the five of you."

"Ugh, I just want this to be over. I'm too old for this shit. I still have so long to go," I groan.

"Four more months is not a long way to go," he laughs. "You were always my toughest little *niña*. What happened?"

"I bumped my head and let someone get me pregnant."

"Someone you love?" my father says softly.

"Maybe," I mumble.

"Why have to turned off your love?" he says more seriously.

I can hear an ache in his voice that throws me back in time. I was such a daddy's girl. We all were. It's why we used to cling to him and tried to be just like him. Not one of us picked up our mother's Jamaican accent.

It's probably because we've mimicked Papi from the time we could say our first words. I remember always wanting to be where he was. Until...

"You broke my heart," I whisper.

"Oh, *cariño*, I never meant for that to happen. To this day, I've wanted to find the words to tell you how sorry I am for what I put you in the middle of," he chokes out.

"How could you do that to us?"

"Your mother was pregnant. We struggled with you girls as it was. I wasn't ready to have another baby, but then I thought I'd finally get that boy," he says wistfully.

"I started out placing a bet here, winning a card game there. I was hot. A friend offered me a chance at some big money. I didn't realize the opportunity was with really bad guys until it was too late.

"Your mother lost the baby because she was stressed about how we were going to pay for things. At the same time, I lost my winning streak. I had to come up with that money. I didn't know what to do," he says.

"And then they came for me," I say.

"*Sí*, I didn't know they did. You ran away and we were so distraught. Losing the baby and then you. I did everything I could to keep you girls happy and healthy. I didn't understand. Not until my problems disappeared.

"You were always my problem solver. The first to get the fight started and to finish it. I should have known from the beginning," he snorts.

"I made sure they never fucked with us again," I say feeling like a small girl and hearing it in my voice.

"But that wasn't your place, *Mi hija*. I would have figured something out," he says.

"Not after what Nelson and I did to those men. They were coming for us. They were going to kill me and Nelson. I was so scared when they jumped me. When Nelson showed up to help, I cut that one guy up bad. I just kept cutting and fighting," I say as the tears fall.

"It was going to end badly if I didn't get help. This wasn't going to be the Marques brawling in the streets like we used to do. I needed to get us real help."

"So you married a —"

"Don't Papi. Whatever you call him, you have to call me. I don't regret my choices. I always do what I have to do. Cristóbal has always been there for me.

"He helped me when he didn't have to. He has always been straight with me," I say defiantly and lift my chin.

"Where I have not. Fine, fair enough. I didn't feel I had to tell my *niñas* my business. You were young girls. But you... you always thought you were a woman.

"I'm being straight with you now, Detra. You have to let love in again," he says pointing to my stomach. "That little one will need it. Your sisters need it."

"I love my sisters," I say, and poke my lip out. "I'll love my baby too."

"And your husband?"

"What about him?"

"When will you let him in and love him?"

"I already let him in. I love Cristó," the words are out before I can trap them in. "Shit."

"*Sí*," my father chuckles and nods behind me.

I turn to find Cristó with a huge smile on his face. My mother and sisters are bouncing behind him. I wiggle my way out of my seat with my five month swollen belly that popped out of nowhere just last week.

One minute it was a tiny bump then poof my waistline was gone. Papi helps me get to my feet. I look at him in confusion then back to Cristó and the rest of my family.

"I have waited years for you to admit that," Cristó says, his eyes suspiciously misting.

"So you sent my father in here to trick me?"

"No." He shakes his head. "He was supposed to bring you the basket."

"Yeah, way to go Papi," Jada says.

"The basket?"

I turn to see the Easter basket Papi placed on the table when he came in. I was too busy being moody to take note of it. It's spilling over with jelly beans, gummy bears, and my favorite caramel Easter eggs. Nestled in the center is a velvet egg shaped box.

"Open it," Cristó says in my ear.

I jump not realizing he crossed the room to get so close. His hands splay my belly as I reach for the velvet egg. I open the box to find a huge blue sapphire and diamond ring.

"What—"

"Will you marry me?" he whispers before nuzzling my neck.

"We're already married," I reply and turn to face him. "And having a baby."

"Humor an old man. Marry me again. I want to hear you say you love me when I pledge my life to you."

"If I humor an old man, what will I do with you?"

He crushes my lips and devours me in front of my family. I try not to whimper, but I can't help tossing my arms around his neck. When he breaks the kiss, his eyes are glowing with joy and mirth.

"Always challenging me. This is why I remain young. *¿Te quieres casar conmigo?*"

"*Sí,* I will marry you," I say with a huge smile. "Cristó?"

"*Sí, Esposita.*"

"*Te amo.*"

"*Te amo, mi amor.* I've loved you for a very long time."

~B~

Cristóbal

"I don't want a nap, Mommy," my wife whines and shoos her mother away.

She is more beautiful with each day. Her nose has spread and her lips seem fuller. Her breasts have swollen as well.

Everything about pregnancy agrees with Detra even if she hates it. Which I know she doesn't. She's in love with our little niño that I intend to spoil just like its mother.

My life is wherever they are. Which means, I haven't been home in months. Manny decided to take his family to Puerto Rico for a little break and reset.

A lot has been reset. I've changed. Trading in more of my old empire for the one my wife has built for me. Enough for us to both take a step back, but not enough to lose my power, respect, and connections, but not before as my wife would say, making an example.

My phone rings and I smile. It's Manny. I want to ask him to be my best man again. This time for a real wedding.

"*Hola*," I answer.

Alarm bells go off as he fires off rapid Spanish. Manny speaks mostly English unless something is wrong or he is upset. Even I am having a hard time following him at the moment.

"She's gone," he finally says and it's the most I understand.

"I'm on my way."

ACKNOWLEDGMENTS

Are you laughing at me? I know it's March. Rolling on the floor. Here's the thing though. This series goes beyond Valentine's Day. I hope you are starting to see we are building up to something here. These may be my break state books where I get to laugh and take a breather, but it's leading somewhere bigger.

Thank you so much for your support. I love what I do. If you only knew how hard I'm working in the background to share my passion with you. Trust me, it's like a Blue Christmas, you can't see what I'm doing, but on Blue Christmas morning when you see all of the gifts that just keep coming you will understand. I haven't forgotten any of the series. I'm just working through the plan a book at a time. (Which in truth is more than one at a time at times. Face palm.)

Thank you so, so much for your support as I take my time with each book and the vision for the series. Thank you for the emails and social media posts. I appreciate them all. This has been an exciting time and a trying one as well. Learning balance has been the biggest obstacle but I'm overcoming it. Your kind words help that more than you know.

Thank you to my other half. Each book has your help and support and I appreciate that so much. To live in the house with crazy... Ha! You're the truth! Thank you so much.

I'm still in awe of God. I know He has so much more in store. I humble myself to not only listen and follow, but to also enjoy the blessings. Too often we get lost in the process and forget to enjoy the fruits of Favor and Grace. I want to say thank you, Lord, and count the blessings with joy!

On to the Next!! *See what happened was… I'm moving to someone you've been asking for. After all there is a plan.*

ABOUT THE AUTHOR

Blue Saffire, award-winning, bestselling author of over thirty contemporary romance novels and novellas—writes with the intention to touch the heart and the mind. Blue hooks, weaves, and loops multiple series, keeping you engaged in her worlds. Every word is meant to have a lasting touch that leaves you breathless for more.

Blue and her husband live in a home filled with laughter and creativity, in Long Island, NY. Both working hard to build the Blue brand and cultivate their love for the arts. Creativity is their family affair.

Wait, there is more to come! You can stay updated with my latest releases, learn more about me, the author, and be a part of contests by subscribing to my newsletter at www.BlueSaffire.com

If you enjoyed Be My Valentine, I'd love to hear your thoughts and please feel free to leave a review. And when you do, please let me know by emailing me TheBlueSaffire@gmail.com or leave a comment on Facebook https://www.facebook.com/BlueSaffireDiaries or Twitter @TheBlueSaffire

Other books by Blue Saffire

Placed in Best Reading Order

Also available....

Legally Bound

Legally Bound 2: Against the Law

Legally Bound 3: His Law

Perfect for Me

Hush 1: Family Secrets

Ballers: His Game

Brothers Black 1: Wyatt the Heartbreaker

Legally Bound 4: Allegations of Love

Hush 2: Slow Burn

Legally Bound 5.0: Sam

Yours: Losing My Innocence 1

Yours 2: Experience Gained

Yours 3: Life Mastered

Ballers 2: His Final Play

Legally Bound 5.1: Tasha Illegal Dealings

Brothers Black 2: Noah

Legally Bound 5.2: Camille

Legally Bound 5.3 & 5.4 Special Edition

Where the Pieces Fall

Legally Bound 5.5: Legally Unbound

Brothers Black 4: Braxton the Charmer

My Funny Valentine

Broken Soldier

Remember Me

Brothers Black 5: Felix the Brain

A Home for Christmas

Coming Soon...

Ballers 3: His Team

Brothers Black 6: Ryan the Joker

Brothers Black 7: Johnathan the Fixer

Road to Whatever Series (Perfect for Me): Ideal For Me Book 2

Blue Saffire Exclusive on the BlueSaffire.com Site

The Lost Souls MC Series

Forever

Never

Always coming soon...

The A Million to Blow Series

A Million to Blow

A Million to Stay

Other books from Evei Lattimore Collection

Books by Blue Saffire

Black Bella 1

Destiny 1: Life Decisions

Destiny 2: Decisions of the Next Generation

Destiny 3 coming soon

Star